W9-AHH-902

4

PRAISE FOR AWARD-WINNING AUTHOR TOM PICCIRILLI!

AFTER ALL THESE YEARS

The horse hadn't even gotten up to a trot before Priest heard a stagecoach ahead of him, coming into town late. A woman's giggling shriek slashed through the quiet rain, and even the roan looked up. One of the canvas curtains parted, letting out a thin ray of lamplight that lit the black words painted across three planks nailed together:

WELCOME TO PATIENCE.

A man laughed.

Priest looked up into the coach's lighted window, seeing a woman's hand turning palm out, revealing one side of her smiling face.

An empty bottle of whiskey flew from the coach and brushed over the roan's left ear. The drapes closed again. Priest reined the horse to a stop and listened to the stage splash through the mud and down into town, until there was only stillness except for the wind. He sighed deeply and didn't move.

The man's voice, that bark of malevolence.

Priest began to tremble.

"My god."

It had been Yuma Dean.

TOM PICCIRILLI

Grave Men

LEISURE BOOKS NEW YORK CITY

For le petite lapin
*to Michelle for her faith and love
and to Don D'Auria, a good friend along this weird and
winding trail*

A LEISURE BOOK®

March 2002

Published by

Dorchester Publishing Co., Inc.
276 Fifth Avenue
New York, NY 10001

ISBN 0-8439-4979-1

The name "Leisure Books" and the stylized "L" with design are trademarks of Dorchester Publishing Co., Inc.

Printed in the United States of America.

Visit us on the web at www.dorchesterpub.com.

Chapter One

Priest snapped awake in his seat, reaching for his knife. He had a mouth full of blood from biting his tongue, and the taste only reminded him of murder. In the nightmare he'd been tied to the chair next to his mother's corpse again, watching his twelve-year-old sister shoot it out with Spider Rafe.

They still got bad sometimes, the dreams, but not so often anymore. Since he'd cut back on his liquor he could almost get a full night's sleep, but these siestas always brought the ugly memories on. Usually he could fight through them and didn't wake up with his heart squeezing through his ribs. This was different. Maybe the sawdust in the air drew him back, or the clouds of bluebottle flies swimming after the dogs in the alley. Maybe he just missed his sister.

The burning high August winds continued to beat at the town, laying down a heavy hand of heat that became a fist at around two in the afternoon, clenching until you wanted to throw yourself in the river.

Priest tried to shrug his thoughts off. He got the feeling that somebody was saying his name close by. Resheathing the blade, he looked to the back of the shop, wondering what might be rushing toward him now, and checked to see if it had already come through the back door. Shadows twined among the empty shelves and he heard his name again, this time in his father's voice.

It got like that on occasion. He stared out through the open front door and caught sight of Chicorah, oldest son of Sondeyka, one of the Apache subchiefs, coming up main street with three of his braves, bringing Gramps back home again.

Now he could hear the stamp of horses, and the murmurs of Gramps as the old man argued with the Apaches in their own tongue, getting nowhere with them. Gramps, as usual when he came back from one of these journeys, wore a grimace of general disdain and spoke only Apache. Chicorah kept up his noncommittal grin, but Gramps scowled, almost pouting, becoming whiter by the minute.

Despite the treaties, there were men in Patience who'd draw down on any Apache who dared jump the rez and enter town. Priest checked the boardwalks and nearby rooftops. Nobody had noticed yet. He glanced around the store and figured he might as well get it over with, he'd just been waiting for something to happen anyway. He stepped outside.

One of Chicorah's men, Delgadito, was a Chevelon Creek Mescalero, and the other two bucks appeared to be Mimbrenos. Once the Chiracahuas would have attacked the other Apache clans as soon as settlers, but Sondeyka had adapted better than most of the chiefs before him. Delgadito had been a scout for the army, and he still carried a Burnside .54 carbine. The others had their Winchesters laid against the pommels of their saddles, pointed straight up. You stuck a couple thousand Apaches together from the six main tribes and you couldn't tell what kind of bonds were being forged up there on White Mountain, who might be starving and who was still singing to the ghost of Cochise.

Gramps stank of mescal, but the old man's eyes were clear. He seemed angry, but resigned to the fact that they were giving him back to Priest again. He wore a breechcloth and a buckskin shirt much too large for his thin, loose-skinned frame, and his sporadic month-long forays into San Carlos had given him a red-mud-colored, leathery look. Nobody knew why Son-deyka's people had taken such a shine to Gramps, but at least they hadn't killed the crazy coot so far.

Chicorah kept his hair even longer than most Apaches, curled and looped in fanciful waves the way Hickok wore his, as an open invitation for anyone man enough to try to scalp him. Fifteen or twenty years ago, when Mangas Coloradas and Cochise led Apacheria, an Indian scalp had been worth two hundred dollars. Ranchers who'd fallen on hard times used to go after Mex scalps just as quickly. Mexicans were farmers tied to their land, easy to find, and nobody could really tell the difference anyway.

Chicorah inspected Priest calmly. "You want blood."

"I just had a nightmare," Priest said. "Nothing personal."

Chicorah knew some of the troubles that ran around inside Priest's skin, and he nodded sagely. "You have a store."

So he was going to get into it. Priest steeled himself as best he could, even though it wouldn't work with Chicorah. "Yes."

"An empty store."

"That's true, for the moment. I just finished putting the shelves in today."

Actually, most of them had been done for ten days, but he'd gotten the last countertop sanded this morning. He'd taken it slow, wanting to stay busy, but there wasn't any point to it now. Lamarr had been gone three weeks. That meant he'd gambled most of the goods money away and whored and drunk the rest of it.

Down the street, buckboards and carriages bustled by. Priest heard women laughing, and boys yelling behind the livery. The tension kept growing, and he couldn't be sure if it was only within him as usual, or if it had finally bled to the outside. Nobody was looking this way.

"It'll be the largest general store in town, where you can find anything you need," he said. The words came to an abrupt end in his throat and stayed there.

Contemplating this, the four Apaches and Gramps all swung back a bit in their saddles as they studied the sign above. Their gazes glided over the plate-glass front window and mounds of sawdust drifting in the dirt. Priest tried not to sigh. Chicorah pulled a cigar out of his shirt, one of a handful he'd gotten from the territorial government men who brought the beef up to the rez. He sniffed at the tobacco, struck a match, and lit it.

Delgadito went a little further, showing he knew the score and wasn't about to let Priest waste their time with any kind of deception. He actually pinched his chin and squinted as if thinking hard. "Where are the many goods that will fill this large place? All those shelves and counters and tables?"

"My partner's bringing them down from Haloosa Creek by wagon tomorrow."

"The big black?"

"That's right. Lamarr."

Beaming now, Delgadito was thinking of Lamarr fondly. Delgadito had once wrestled Lamarr in White Canyon and lost, and ever since he'd sort of loved him for it. You could never tell with Apaches. Step across their trail by accident and they'd hang you upside down over a bonfire; or you could kill seventeen of them while defending a water hole and they'd call you a friend for life.

"If you gave the big black your money, it is because you did not want it."

That, too, was true in its own fashion, but Priest kept silent.

Gramps got off the sorrel, taking nothing tied to the horse, including the Springfield in the saddle boot. He came over to Priest and stood there with his head hanging. The others got down from their horses as well, slowly, playing it out. They were getting a real kick out of this, the Mimbrenos braves starting to chuckle a little. Priest kept checking the street, watching a few passing coaches, the odd glances of lone riders, but nobody concerned enough to stop.

Chicorah stepped up close and stared at Priest for a while, leaning forward so they could get deep into each other's face. The Apache kept grinning beneath his natural fury, but mostly there was only disappointment.

He eventually turned to Delgadito, who dropped the barrel of his Burnside, aiming low. Priest frowned through it all. Delgadito almost seemed embarrassed, shocked that he was doing what he was doing. This wasn't his way. He walked until he was in the doorway of the shop, drew down on the lamp beside the chair, and pulled the trigger. Kerosene splashed everywhere against the finely sanded pine shelving.

Chicorah puffed on his cigar one more time, letting Priest know what was coming. Giving him plenty of time to react if he really wanted to.

Priest just stood there, his shoulder muscles relaxing for the first time in weeks. Chicorah tossed his cigar down and they all stood back and watched the place go up.

Flames erupted and the front window fractured and blew out in less than a minute. Priest didn't work glass very well, but he had thought he'd done better than this. Now he saw how mistaken he was. Anybody could tell what a roughshod job he'd done.

The fire spilled higher, with spirals of smoke twirling in the wind. Some of the pine was so fresh he could smell the bubbling sap. The heated air caused the sawdust at their feet to first course one way and then the other.

For Chicorah to burn a mercantile store—even an empty one—while Apaches died up in San Carlos waiting for the government agents to deliver pathetic amounts of beef and blankets, showed just how far out on the edge he was. No wonder he and Gramps got along so well.

"You have a larger fate than this," Chicorah said. "Your mother and father need no food."

Priest made a strangled noise like he'd taken a whip across the eyes.

It was almost going a step too far, and Chicorah seemed to realize it. He braced himself, and Delgadito and the other two bucks kept their eyes on Priest's blade. Even Gramps lifted his chin.

Flames warmed Priest's back and the smoke billowed around him as if something inside of himself were being burned out. Chicorah was too polite to call Priest a coward, but the Apache had just come damn close. Honor meant more now than ever before, as it was stolen inch by inch along with everything else.

Priest tried to match Chicorah's smile but knew he looked insane doing it. His breath came in bites, and he heard his father say his name again. He drew his lips together into a bloodless wrinkled line. Then he let it pass, as he did most things.

Chicorah put his hand on Priest's shoulder and said, "We have all made too many bad mistakes these last few years. It is time for you to stop making yours."

They all remounted, and Priest and Gramps watched the horses trot up the street, in no hurry at all, nobody giving them a backward glance. Chicorah didn't like cigars anyway, and tossed his into the dust.

The fire soon swallowed the store, rising in gushes to surge at the sign above: McCLAREN & RUSSELL. Lamarr had never much liked the sign, arguing that his name should go up top, what with him being the first Negro to own even half a shop in Patience. It had taken Priest a week to properly carve the letters and seal the wood. Flames chewed at the words until the paint bubbled and spit down into the street. A lot of people had gathered around to watch as the roof started to cave in.

He stared after the Apaches, feeling free of his

parents' dreams for the first time in years as the comfortable weight of his remorse sank on him once again. He turned his face to the blaze and muttered, "Thanks."

Whispering behind him, like a rustle of feather and leaf, Gramps—only an old white man now, dressed in a silly getup and dragging his skinny ass, looking around with a tear-streaked, dirty face—said it, too. "Thank you. Oh, my brothers, thank you."

Chapter Two

They could've at least made a show of it instead of just staring and passing small talk, telling jokes and spinning parasols on their shoulders, with Mrs. Henderson offering lemonade off her front porch.

The townspeople of Patience didn't rally with water buckets, because most of the neighbors knew Priest wasn't really going to make much of a go with the store anyway. Besides, right across the alley was Tolliver's Mercantile, and a few streets over you had Hasseler's General Store, and on the other side of town stood Freerson's Dry Goods Emporium, all of which had stocked Patience for the thirty-five years since the town had been settled. Moreover, none of them came from an insane family or partnered with a big ex-slave who claimed he used to get drunk with Abe Lincoln.

Priest heard the mumbles and angry whispers. "That's what a nigger lover gets. Only a matter of time 'fore somebody burned 'em out." Priest laughed it off, because none of them had the salt to say it to Lamarr's face, or even to his own. At least things were shaking out, and soon he could get on with his business, whatever that might be.

By the time the ashes had settled and folks began wandering off, Gramps was lying in a ball near the livery trough, scaring the horses. Sheriff Amos Burke sauntered over and took in the scene with a smirk, hoping that Priest was finally on the way to becoming either a lawman or a full-fledged outlaw, just so long as he did some damn thing. Priest was sort of hoping Chicorah would come back and tell him a little more about destiny, and give him some kind of a hint of what the hell he should do now.

Burke put a little extra swagger into his walk now, expecting the embers of the store to throw enough light to glint against his badge, his bottom gold teeth, and those polished spurs. He wanted it to give him a rosy-dusk glow like he'd just stepped out of the sunset. He tried to keep his eyes steady, but he couldn't help glancing around to see if anybody in the remaining crowd was watching him.

Women tittered softly, and several children played hide-and-seek at the other end of the alley. Some of the whores, awakened by the noise, stepped out onto the porch of Miss Patty's. The Christian Ladies Coalition scurried across the street and made prune faces, reciting scripture as the sunlight started to fade.

Burke kept posing, showing off his profile first to the left side and then the right. He'd long been an admirer of Susan Murdock, the mayor's wife, who stood nearby up on the boardwalk. He'd also ached for Miss Patty, the whorehouse madam who was younger than most of her girls, and he actually blushed in her presence. Both ladies took a lot of impressing, though, and Burke didn't have enough distinction, charm, or money to cause much of a fuss.

Still, Susan Murdock urged him on as usual, licking her lips while the mayor pointed toward the trough and wrinkled his nose at Gramps. Miss Patty, staring down from her balcony, met Priest's gaze and gave him a wink. They both understood what was coming.

Here it was. Burke notched up his strut, really throwing his hips. His brown suit was freshly pressed, and his bow tie had been perfectly centered under his collar. His thick mustache leaned too far to the left, and he cocked his head to that side as if he were about to be pulled over. He stopped in front of Priest and, much louder than necessary, said, "Priest McClaren, don't you go running off. You hear? You just set right there. I want words with you."

As if Priest were sneaking away with stolen bags of bank money and Burke had caught him dead in his tracks.

Priest wasn't going anywhere, sitting in the dirt. Gramps, coming back into the world a bit, called *"Ethel, Ethel,"* and pawed the wet ground beneath the trough. Grandmother had been gone almost ten years, but at least the old man was having white thoughts again.

Priest stared at Burke for a while, wondering what it would be like to be the sheriff of Patience. Maybe have Lamarr as his deputy, both of them with badges on their vests, strutting around chuckholes, tipping their hats, and saying, "How do?" all the time. He could imagine getting soft in the neck and belly, and trying to find enough wax to keep his mustache from drooping too far to the east. Priest thought it might be worthwhile to never have to pick up a knife again.

Mayor Frederick Murdock, who rarely strung five words together at a time except during an election, put a hand on Priest's shoulder and said, "Perhaps you'll consider farming now, Mr. McClaren."

"Farming?"

"Farming is important to the survival of our community. We need more farmers." He'd gotten so used to saying pleasant, meaningless things that it no longer mattered to him whether they made any sense. "You've strong hands. You would do well with farming."

Priest looked around at the red sandstone hills, lava spikes and greasewood, prickly pear and saguaro and Joshua trees, the desolate waste of the boundless alkali flats. He said, "Thanks for your faith in me, Freddy."

The mayor smiled happily at that and walked off arm in arm with his wife. Susan Murdock looked backward over her shoulder at the sheriff, who glowered after her, his Adam's apple bobbing wildly. His scowl brought his brow low enough so that it nearly touched the curled tips of his mustache. Susan wiggled her backside, really pouring on the effect, and the boys in the alley stopped playing so they could watch. Priest thought it might be funny to see Burke tonight, staring into his mirror, washing his face, and mystified at how he'd gotten wax in his eyebrows. Priest stood up.

Burke said, "We got word that your sister put

down Sarsaparilla Sam in Santa Fe two weeks ago. Eleven hundred dollars."

"Sarsaparilla Sam?" The hell was the world coming to when they paid over a thousand for a killer called Sarsaparilla Sam? "You mean some idiot really went by that name?"

"It's a bad joke, because he dry-gulches the teetotaling drinkers and settlers coming in from the East. His real name is Samuel Wade."

Oh, Wade. The one who liked to find lone adobes built by families fresh to the West, thinking they could start some kind of a new life out of the cities. Clerks and their wives, two or three children with at least one young girl, maybe around thirteen years old. Wade liked making the girls watch their homes burn down, showing them what he could do to her parents and brothers with his lasso.

Molly must've had a hell of a lot of bloody fun with him before she'd taken him down.

"From what they're reporting, it was ugly. Unduly ugly. She did him pretty raw, McClaren."

"Good."

"Do you know what you're saying?"

Ashes washed over his boots, and Gramps cried out for Grandmother again, his hands like claws scratching at the underside of the trough. "Yes, I know what I'm saying."

"You wouldn't think it was so funny if you knew the details."

"I don't think it's funny."

They'd gone around like this many times before, nearly word for word. Sheriff Amos Burke always lost his composure at about this point, and his voice started to climb a little higher. Part of it had to do with the fact that Burke had never seen blood outside of his own shaving nicks, and also because he thought Molly was sending back wads of reward money to Priest. It put him in the position of being envious, embarrassed, and resentful all in one nasty bundle.

"Sheriff in Santa Fe said she left headed in this direction, and that she's pretty heavy with child. She might be coming home to Patience."

His sister Molly pregnant? He tried to imagine it but couldn't bull past the fact that she wasn't even eighteen yet, no matter how long she'd been on her own. "She won't be back to stay."

"You so sure of that?"

He wasn't, but he couldn't imagine she'd return.

"It's not natural for a woman, I tell you." Burke spoke in a booming voice as if he were giving a sermon, trying to reach the back pews. "Living the life she does. Christ . . . Woman—she's not yet a woman, a girl her age, for God's sake, doing what she's doing."

23

"Natural enough for her," Priest said, knowing it was true.

"Don't you have any feelings at all, man? His body was—"

"Good."

"You're not letting me finish. If you'd listen you might realize that something should be done."

"You're right, and she's doing it."

"No no, that's not what I mean. So just listen. He'd been—"

Priest didn't need to have another picture painted for him. "He deserved it."

"Ethel, Ethel."

With an absurd growl, the sheriff gave it up for the moment, toed the dirt, and checked over at Gramps. "That old man is sick. Sick in his brain." Burke skinned back his upper lip. He'd been working on his sneer again. He was getting a lot better at it, figuring out just how far he had to raise his upper lip to get it out from under the mustache. "And I fear you're heading in the same direction. One of these days you're going to go mad in the streets, tearing out your own eyes and stinking in your own shit."

It was a definite possibility. "If it happens like that, I'll do my best to stay away from the good churchgoing folks and stick to the back alleys."

"I'll help take you down. It'll be my pleasure, let me tell you."

Priest inspected the sneer and said, "Pretty nice, Amos, but you still need a little more practice. You aren't peeling your smile back quite enough—it's catching on some of those rotted teeth."

"Why, you lousy son of a bitch."

A breeze kicked up around them, like tiny hands pushing. There was a moment when it could've gone either way, and they both knew it. Burke dropped his hand toward his gunbelt and hedged backward, looking for some extra room. Priest took one step forward, which put him too close to draw on.

Burke's eyes clouded as he puzzled out whether he should take another step backward and try it again, or if Priest would just move in on him once more. He glanced down at Priest's belt to see if the knife was still there. He didn't see it, and didn't see Priest's right hand either.

How'd it happen like that, so fast, without any sound?

While he was staring, realizing too late that Priest had the knife and could open him up wide in three seconds, Burke decided to live another day and let it pass.

But the sheriff had learned to take some advice. This time the sneer was a lot cleaner, much sharper. "At least my sister isn't the only one with guts in my family. Tell me, what's it like knowing she's out there avenging your dead parents while you're sitting here with a crazy fool at your feet, a drunk smart-mouthed nigger for a partner, and so broke you can't even rub two fifty-cent pieces together?"

Priest considered it seriously, wondering how Burke's rage might match up to his own. They'd have to see, one of these days. "Probably not a lot worse than being in love with two women and not getting so much as a kiss or a kind word from either of them. Then again, I'm not really sure. What are your thoughts on the subject?"

"You bastard, I ought to—"

"No, you really shouldn't."

"Ethel, Ethel."

Priest could reach over and yank the star off Burke's coat, make a fair wage, and maybe even find a wife to keep his house. Have Gramps live in a room in the attic, or maybe out back in a shed. Someplace where he could sing Apache songs and not bother anybody. Give his sister Molly a guest room big enough for her trunk of rifles and pistols, all the saddlebags full of bounty money. Plenty of tacks so she could hang all the Wanted posters up side by side and study the faces of the men she went after. Lamarr might dry out long enough to handle a steady job, save a little money, quit fighting the long-dead Confederacy. Priest could try not to wake everybody up when he got the shrieking fits in the middle of the night—

"What the hell you gaping at, McClaren?" Burke asked.

—maybe even invite Chicorah over to the house, along with the *Ga'ns* mountain spirits Sondeyka said lived inside Priest. He could introduce them around to his wife and her friends at their tea parties, everybody shaking hands and eating finger sandwiches, kids laughing everywhere, one big happy family.

"I asked what you're staring at!"

Priest walked away from the sheriff without another word, leaving Burke seething there and spitting out the now drooping ends of his mustache. Priest picked Gramps up, carried him to Miss Patty's, and put the old man to bed upstairs in the whorehouse.

Chapter Three

Despite all the cigar smoke in the air, Priest could still smell only burning pine. Patty gave him a cockeyed grin and didn't charge him for the room. They'd talk more later, he knew, but for now she let him slide on past the working girls.

Music and noise shook the walls, and Priest could almost let himself go with it, if he wanted to. He didn't. Gramps would sleep through the night and most of tomorrow, his sixty-seven white years catching up to him.

Priest checked his grandfather over carefully for marks and scars but found nothing new. Apaches took care of their kin.

The night kept getting hotter. Priest took off

his shirt, washed up in the basin on a pedestal table covered in a lace shawl, and lit a cigarette. His wet hair hung in his eyes, and he checked the mirror to make sure he'd gotten all the soot off. He was twenty-three and already going gray, a couple of silver-tinged curls right out in front. He stood in the window looking down at the scorched spot where the store would've been, feeling the wind sweep against his chest. Any usable timber would probably be carted off during the night and show up across town where they were putting up new buildings every month. He turned down the lamp until it was almost dark in the room and smoked three more cigarettes. When his hair dried, he washed up again and put his shirt back on.

He opened the cedar chest at the foot of the bed and dug beneath poorly folded blankets and sheets. Priest kept a spare change of clothes for Gramps in here, and he wished that the old man would get in the mood to take off his clothes and put on a breechcloth before he went Apache, instead of just running up to White Mountain with whatever he was wearing, leaving the clothes scattered across the cliffs. Priest laid out his grandfather's pants and shirt, the black suspenders and his tie, a pipe, tobacco, and a pair of worn but polished shoes.

A faint sound in the hall made him turn. Patty

let herself in and stood in the doorway with an uncorked bottle of whiskey and two glasses. "You look like you could use a drink."

"I always look that way," Priest said. "But no thanks."

That surprised her, and she pursed her lips. Priest rarely turned down whiskey, but he didn't want to lose the feeling that he was on the verge of change, that something else would break soon and set him on a different course.

"Francine will take care of your grandfather. I figured you didn't want to be stuck here all night. She'll be up in a few minutes and check on him every couple hours or so."

"I appreciate that."

"And when she's busy, I'll do it."

"Thanks. He always said you were sweet on him."

"I am, I suppose." She grinned, and the dimples came through. His heart hitched to one side, picking up speed, and he wanted to sweep a few stray hairs from her forehead. He lifted his hand a couple inches and let it down again.

"He was always nice to me," she said. "Even when I was a girl. He used to put apple blossoms in his hair and throw pennies to the kids outside the candy store, sing us songs on that three-string guitar of his. He still got that thing?"

"No."

"Well, that's a shame."

Patty stepped closer, her shoulders dappled with sweat. In this light, her hair caught the color of her blue petticoats, and those eyes carried the moon. Her shadow loomed large against his throat, and he kept swallowing. She brought her lips closer and closer still until he nearly leaned in toward her, expecting that familiar taste again. She moved off to his right, leaving him there.

"I know you hate hearing this, but he really should be in a hospital someplace, one of them sanitariums they got in the East."

"That would only kill him."

Her presence pressed against him, and he began to sweat more heavily. The glasses clinked gently, ringing soft notes. There were times he couldn't quite follow her movements, as if she twined amid the darkness, reappearing here and there.

"I wonder why they give him back?" she asked. "Why keep him around for a month or two, teach him their language and songs, only to make him come on home again?"

"He can only handle it so long, then the rest of his whole white life pushes back through. When he starts calling out for my grandmother, Chicorah knows it's time to get him off White Mountain. Any longer than that and he'll start scaring their children."

31

"Padre Villejo would take him in at the mission."

"That would only kill Padre Villejo."

He saw her getting ready to ask, and resigned himself. She said, "Did you set fire to the store?"

"No, see, it was Chicorah, he—"

With almost a tone of indignation, Patty frowned and said, "And you didn't see fit to stop him."

"There were four Apaches, and Gramps was still one of them at the time. Would you see fit to go up against the lot of them?"

"Me? Nope. But you would, of course. You'd go against them and beat them all, if you had reason. You didn't have one, though, now did you?"

He tried to find an excuse why he shouldn't be honest with her, but he couldn't come up with one. "No," he said. "I was glad he did it."

Some folks would have asked why, but Patty knew all there was to know about Priest. Or almost, anyway. There was a long pause that kept on lengthening in the silence, until she started to snicker. He expected it to keep on surging out of her, so he sat on the bed and waited, saying, "All right, okay, let's have it. Go on." She let loose a barking giggle that soon started coming out her nose. It was an ugly sound, but one he didn't really mind. When she tried to swallow the laughter, it just worked on up again. He didn't join her, but that didn't matter. The laugh was on him, but that didn't matter much either.

Finally she started to settle down some.

"You through?" he asked.

"Sorry."

"Don't be. I kind of wondered what was taking so long."

Her breath, whiskey-laden, wafted over him, and he sniffed at it. He stared at her hips, because he always stared at her hips. This wasn't crass or vulgar, but he always felt that way around her now. He couldn't stop remembering how, when they were teenagers, he used to rub the back of his hand over the slick rise of her thigh. He used to know in his heart they'd get married one day, and tell their grandchildren about the cool spring evenings when they'd sit on the porch swing and hold hands like it was the only thing that counted in the world.

Patty's mother had died in childbirth, bearing a stillborn sister, and when she was seventeen her father had died. He had gone down in a mine shaft to check a couple of dynamite charges. A couple of hours later they found half the upper bridge of his false teeth on top of the hoisting cage and part of his skull embedded in an ore cart, and that's all they had to bury. Priest would've married her, except by then his parents were dead and the bottle had swallowed him. He'd always love Miss Patty and would always blame himself for helping her to go the way she did. He should've been stronger, but that was true of everyone.

"What are you thinking about?" she asked.

He smiled and shook his head. Except for a few worry lines at the edges of her eyes, she looked exactly the same as she had the first time he'd slept with her down by the arroyo. "Nothing."

"You're mooning over Sarah again, aren't you?"

He always was, so why not now? "Maybe that's it."

"She singing tonight?"

"Yes."

"You going to see her?"

The burr in her voice caught his attention. It sounded almost like resentment, except Patty didn't have it in her to ever get jealous. She put one glass on the table but kept holding the other and the bottle. She backhanded a black curl off her forehead, and the dim lamplight caught the sheen between her breasts, the cool pale angle of her neck, and perfect rose O of her lips. Keeping the charm turned on all the way because she didn't know how to turn it down anymore. That was all right by him, for the moment. She flashed him those dimples that, as always, made his entrails buck. He spun to one side, hoping she didn't notice how he flinched.

"Yes," he answered. "I'm heading over there in an hour or so. She goes on stage at ten."

"Get there by nine-thirty, and make some noise so she knows you're in the audience. Don't go in skulking the way you usually do. Septemus woos her loudly enough—you better start doing the same. And for God's sake, tell her the fire was an accident and that you're going to rebuild soon."

"She knows me as well as you do, Patty."

"Not quite, I reckon."

He let a hiss of annoyance out between his teeth. "How long do you figure I could keep a lie going when she was looking me straight in the face?"

She didn't even have to think about it. "Ten, twelve seconds, maybe. Well, all right then, if you're not going to lie, then make sure you keep enough money in your pocket for when the hat shop opens in the morning. I've never seen a woman who liked hats as much as she does, and you're going to be shopping for a while. Get something with lots of ribbons."

The millinery, always back to the millinery. He should get there early and let Miss Henshaw the milliner spend most of the day helping him pick out hats and chin ribbons and those big white saucer-shaped sunbonnets that Sarah wore on picnics and to church. Septemus usually bought up half the stock and had it delivered straight to Sarah's home, carriages filled with stacks of hatboxes arriving at all hours, the drivers carrying them in and holding out the silk streamers for her to inspect. Priest had a little faith that he could pick out the one that mattered if he could just get there early enough. He hoped Lamarr would come back with at least a few dollars left. They were going to need it.

"Ethel, Ethel. Thank you, brothers."

Patty's gaze dropped to the old man, and when she set her eyes on Priest again he knew they were almost done talking. That air of change settled again, and Patty must've felt it too. She had two quick shots of whiskey that made the dew at her throat thicken into rolling beads, and then she put the bottle down with a thump.

"I know about Molly down in Santa Fe," she said. "At this rate, she's going to run every other bounty hunter out of business."

"She's good at what she does."

"There's no denying that. How many's that so far? Six? Seven?"

Closer to fifteen over the last three years, but there was no reason to let anybody else know. "Somewhere around that."

"She'll never get rid of all that sorrow, no matter how many of those killers she brings down."

"She's brought a few of them back alive," Priest said.

"To the hangman. You think it's bled off any of that crazy hate she's got inside her? Has she gotten rid of any of it? Do you think you ever will?"

Of course not, but what was the point of heading off on that track now? Priest stood there and stared at her thighs, thinking of the days lying by the arroyo, wondering what time the millinery opened.

Breeze from the window flipped the curl back across her face. She was close enough now that he could brush her hair aside, but he wouldn't be able to let her go with only a slight touch. She knew that, but didn't know him quite as well as she thought, and didn't realize he could grow sentimental for the children they'd been and not only needy for her body.

"Probably not, Patty," he said.

At the sound of her name, which he almost never spoke aloud anymore, she chuckled and shook her head sadly. He could feel the heat of her disappointment and frustration rolling off her in waves as they walked downstairs to the bar.

Chapter Four

Plenty of noise, music, and action going on here, the kind that kept Priest looking around all the time. The stink of conflicting perfumes alone could kick a pack mule over, but it couldn't cover the smell of horseshit, stale beer, and female sweat. Priest sort of liked the enveloping odor, the headiness and intensity of it.

Several of the girls were laughing and dancing with men in the parlor. Priest took a seat and kept his eyes open. Patty went to the kitchen to check on getting him something to eat.

The carousing went on, with Fat Jim playing the piano wildly, coming up halfway out of his seat. Fat Jim tried to liven up the mood, really working his right-hand slide. He weighed about

a hundred and five pounds and barely came up
to the shoulder of most of the girls, but somehow
he still had a potbelly. His dented derby was
yanked down tight on his head, with just a frill
of gray hair showing. His cigar spewed ash across
the keys, and he'd chawed on it so hard during
the song that tobacco juice ran down his chin.
He looked a little slap-happy banging the keys so
hard, knowing it was up to him to make the
atmosphere.

Some of the women were faking their humor
tonight, and their forced laughter came out
stilted and ugly. The cowhands and miners fresh
into town didn't mind at all. Erin just danced to
kill time, and Missy smiled only when somebody
looked at her. That edge in the air kept slicing
down.

A tremor ran through Priest's shoulders, and
he knew something was about to try for his
throat again. Patty returned and sat beside him,
had another whiskey from the bar, and said,
"You think she'll ever catch up with Yuma
Dean?"

Priest sucked air between his teeth. He hadn't
realized she'd been hitting the booze so hard.
He'd never seen her drunk before, and, like him,
she was a quiet and vile one. The liquor might
not be able to bolster your backbone, but it could
get you to saying things you wouldn't dare say in

your right head. Something had gotten under her skin, and he figured he'd just have to wait another minute or two before she let him know what it was.

He believed he could stand it that long. He sat calmly for a moment until the truth abruptly came that, no, he couldn't handle this right now. He didn't want to wait it out, thinking about his murdered parents, and he started to get up and get the hell out of there.

Nobody else, not even Burke or Lamarr or Chicorah, had the brass to mention Yuma Dean's name to Priest's face.

A sloe-eyed redhead came out of the kitchen and slapped a bowl of stew on the bar in front of Priest, but it was already too late. He'd been too slow, lagged too long, and now there was a price to pay for not escaping while he could. Patty took another slug of whiskey, her neck no longer the soft china white, but flushed with an angry dappled red.

"You're a goddamn fool," she said. Even though there were no tears, he understood she was as close to crying as she was ever likely to come anymore.

"Okay," he said.

"You had a chance to make something of your life, cut loose from the past, and get married. Sarah would have you in a minute if you could provide her with a home, but oh no, oh hell no, you just had to go and do an idiotic thing like burning down your own store before you even opened it."

"No, see, it was Chicorah, he—"

He turned and saw the glaze in her eyes, the set of her mouth, uncertain of how they'd come so far from where they'd been upstairs in the room. The music maybe, or the laughter and stink, something here reminding her that the past was too far off to go after again, so you might as well settle into the place you'd made. This was hers.

He didn't say anything, but she waved him off as if he had, swooning a little in her seat. His failures affected her harder than they'd ever hurt him. It came to this sometimes. He stared into the bowl of stew and let the trails of steam swirl and break against his nose. She wheeled and elbowed him in the ribs lightly, then again, harder, and once more until he gave in.

He glanced up so she could look him directly in the eye.

And Christ, she wasn't drunk, not at all, she'd just had enough of him. "I've never seen anyone as full of fear and hate as you."

"All right," he said.

"No one else as terrified at moving on as you, Priest."

41

"Okay," he said.

Now there was a little tenderness as she raised her hand to his cheek and her breath twined around him. "Even Molly's gotten over it in her own way."

"Yes, I know."

"You refuse to even get riled, don't you? Get out of here. Go marry that Sarah O'Brien and move far away from Patience and raise a house full of pups and be happy, much as you can be."

A twenty-three-year-old madam who lived neck-deep in the sweltering summer burn of a desert town, among rowdy men hoping to squeeze out some of their rage between a pair of greasy thighs, surrounded by middle-aged whores with their teeth starting to go, telling him how to get on the right path. "You might want to take some of your own advice, Patty."

"I just might." She grinned then, and everything was exactly as it had been before. "Hell, I just might at that." Patty glided off, encompassed by the swirling skirts of her dress.

Priest got up to leave, but she'd left the bottle behind, and for the first time in three months he seriously considered getting drunk. One sip would lead to the whole bottle, and there wouldn't be any turning back this time. He eased the whiskey away from himself, and in a minute somebody reached out and took it into another

42

swarm of laughter and motion. He forced himself to finish the stew, even though his belly was still knotted. He needed the meal, and he didn't know when or where he'd get his next one.

Fat Jim kept playing, his tiny fingers somehow making the distance to the high F-sharp, one song rolling into another without any break. Someone had stuck a new stogie in his mouth, but it wasn't lit.

Miss Patty's house didn't have a full-length mirror behind the parlor bar, just a rounded one the size of an attic window up high in the corner, facing out on an angle so Patty and Wainwright, the houseman, could keep watch over things. Priest's eyes wandered and he kept checking it, and already he saw trouble reflecting back at him.

It was all part of the challenge of this night, and there wasn't a whole lot he could do. Priest took it in stride, the way such things were meant to be taken, but he was glad the bottle of whiskey was gone. He had a thirst now. He licked his lips.

Wainwright sat perched on his wrought-iron seat against the far wall. He kept his gaze set on two cavalry riders fresh out of the army, men who'd given most of their youth to officers and regulations and didn't have money or home to show for it. Angry bastards who'd as soon shoot one of Patty's girls as an Apache or each other.

They hunkered on a divan, perusing the ladies and finding all of them lacking.

Priest was impressed by their sneers, and wished Burke would walk in right now to see how it was done right. Wainwright nodded to himself, knowing trouble was coming. He turned a sour expression to Priest. Priest tried not to return it but was pretty sure he did. They'd both seen these types before, and the pressure in the room kept growing, though no one else cared.

Wainwright stood six feet five, heading toward three hundred pounds. But because he had a tendency to hunch down some, with the swollen powerful arms hanging heavily at his sides, he gave the impression that he was nearly as wide as he was tall. His respectfully polite attitude put everyone at ease. Even if you might consider him an ugly brute, you'd judge him a docile one.

There was a feral quality to him: He didn't walk so much as he padded and loped. He didn't greet you as much as he allowed you to share his guarded space. You couldn't help but feel comfortable with him. He seemed as much a part of the house as the furniture. As if his wiry steel-gray skullcap of hair, thick high-ridged eyebrows, and deep-set black eyes were just another part of his pressed blue suit, and when he pulled off his coat he would slip off his skin too. Beneath would be a different kind of beast. He cut the most imposing figure of a man in all of Patience, with the possible exception of Lamarr.

His upper body hardly moving as he lumbered past the piano, Wainwright came on over. He said in his snarling but quiet voice, "I heard about the fire. Since you don't look too choked up about it, I'll save my sympathies until you really need them."

"If it's all the same to you, I'll take them now."

"Yeah?"

"I suspect they won't go to waste."

"By all means, then, they're yours for the taking."

"Thanks," Priest said, and somehow he meant it.

"How are you fixed for the near future?"

"That depends on what you mean by the near future."

"The extremely near future," Wainwright said. "As in the present."

Priest hated to admit to his own mistakes. "Well, it's like this. Gramps is upstairs getting white again in his sleep. Lamarr's got all the money and must've spent it on whores and faro by now."

"How long's it been?"

"Three weeks."

"Oh, hell yes, then." Wainwright did his impersonation of laughter, the noise coming out in staggered growls. "So it's gone and you're both broke."

"I fear that's the case."

"I can float you fifty, for a month or two."

The cavalry riders continued to stew as the girls got a bit more raucous with the other men in the parlor. Fat Jim could drown out a lot, but not all of it. Giggles and squeals drifted down through the ceiling from the second and third floors.

"I appreciate the sentiment, but I'll let it pass for the time being. I think this party is about to be ruined."

"Don't you believe it. Excuse me a moment."

"You want some help?" Priest asked. He knew it was the wrong thing to say the second he said it. Sometimes Wainwright could go either way with how seriously he took his job. Still, Priest was hoping Wainwright might let him help out, just this once.

The houseman didn't appear to be offended. "That won't be necessary, but thanks kindly for your offer."

"You're welcome."

Wainwright got to turn out whatever went on inside him at least a couple times a week, on average. You could always find somebody coming into the house who couldn't feel good about himself unless he was roughing up a woman, or a bitter drunk who wanted to shoot up the place for laughs. You'd see a boy who'd been taken at poker at the saloon and lost all his family's money. Some of those kids just wanted to lay their heads against a soft breast before trying to hang themselves from the third-floor banister.

Others wanted to go out in a bloodbath. Wainwright handled them all with little fuss. He once came downstairs with two unconscious cowboys, one under each arm, a couple of rough riders wanted for holding up a stagecoach in Cheyenne. He'd left a third bushwhacker dead on the second floor with two snapped ribs piercing his heart.

He assessed the situation instantly. Wainwright looked down and spun past one of the cavalrymen in a single flowing action. He realized that no matter how scornful the bastard might be, his mustache filled with foam from pouting in his beer, brooding because even the fat whores with dimpled asses had comfortable beds and more money than he had himself, the yahoo would just mope and drink himself into oblivion.

The other one was different. His rage ran off him in coils that snapped at everybody in the room. He was already coming out of his chair and reaching toward Erin, maybe to smash her teeth in or just to yank her out of the cowhand's arms. The rider let out a yelp of disgust as his fists grappled for the girl but closed on air. Wainwright, looking fairly bored, had him by the collar.

The music kept going, and so did the laughter and dancing and drinking, as the guy's eyes got wide and he went for his Colt. The sound of the pistol beginning to clear leather was loud, but it was almost lost beneath the grotesque noise of breaking bone.

Slick, all right. Wainwright covered the cavalryman's mouth with his massive left hand so nobody would have to be bothered listening to him screech. The muffled screams didn't get past Wainwright's hairy bulbous knuckles. His right fist tightened further and crushed the cavalryman's fingers—still wrapped around the pistol—until the blood came leaking across the barrel, his face turning a nice shade of purple.

Only Fat Jim saw it all, and he just kept on playing. Nobody else noticed, not even the guy's partner, who continued to sulk and mutter to himself at the table. Erin and the cowhand kissed and swept each other around the settee, heading for one of the bedrooms. Wainwright drifted backward quickly, almost gliding across the carpet, with the cavalryman's toes barely touching the floor as he was dragged away and vanished out the back.

Francine came down the stairs, spotted Priest, and said, "I just checked your grandpa. He's still out cold. But what do I do if he wakes up screaming?"

"He won't."

"How do you know? I don't want to listen to him if he starts going crazy. Didn't I hear Patty say he sometimes wakes up in the middle of the night shrieking his throat raw?"

"No," Priest said. "No. That's me."

Chapter Five

Lights of the Home Hearth Theater blazed upon a stage filled with frightened birds and a half-naked magician's assistant. She jiggled in all the right places and a few of the wrong ones, too. She ran after the hopping birds, trying not to step on them. Their wings had been clipped and they swung around in wide circles: magpies dyed yellow with their tail feathers plucked out.

The magician stood in the audience with his cape swirling in the draft, asking a miner to choose cards from an oversized deck. Priest watched from the back for a few minutes but couldn't make out what the trick was supposed to be. Nobody else cared, either. They were drunk and laughing, and every time the assistant came to the edge of the stage clutching magpies to her chest, somebody would slap her in the ass and they'd all cheer.

Septemus Hart sat in his seat of honor in the balcony, sipping sherry and dressed in black trousers and vest with a purple shirt. He wore a gray rebel coat with gold epaulets, medals, and tassels on it. He'd been a captain in the Confederate army and still enjoyed dressing up and showing off the chevrons on his sleeve, using his hanging drawl of an accent when it benefited him as a good ole boy. Septemus owned the theater and about a third of the rest of Patience. New construction was going on every day, and Septemus had a hand in almost all of it.

He did his best to appear regal and debonair, but Griff, the left-handed gunny always at his side, sort of ruined the impression. Septemus was forever polished and refined, smiling and chuckling and trying to make eye contact with folks, while Griff gave everyone a dead-cold stare.

Griff hadn't been on the trail in five years, but still he looked like he'd just come in from the desert. No matter what happened, he'd never draw unless Septemus was in danger. Someday, though, Lamarr would push Septemus too far, or vice versa, and Griff would make a move and then Priest would move, and there'd be blood shed all over the damn place.

The fact was, Lamarr couldn't kill the old man until Septemus admitted aloud to being Lamarr's daddy, and Septemus just didn't seem like he was ever going to oblige him.

Priest waited for Sarah O'Brien to take the stage.

The magician took his bows, and the assistant stumbled off, clutching the magpies amid a spattering of rowdy hoots and boot stomps. The Home Hearth Theater was like a saloon on occasion, and at other times like an opera house. You could find a little of everything here over the course of a week. Priest looked around and spotted the cowpokes, ranch scouts, the easterners, the well-bred, and the bewildered drunkards who kept waiting for the girls to take their clothes off. Patience had been growing at such a rate that the number of new faces in town sometimes took him back a step. Three years ago, he could name nearly everyone he passed on the street the whole day. Now he knew hardly anybody at all.

Septemus had been expanding the borders and putting up so many buildings that carpenters, mill men, and architects came from as far away as New Hampshire looking for a chance to make better pay in a swelling city. The Home Hearth itself had once been little more than a twenty-foot stage and a few seats before Septemus turned it into a damn near coliseum with space for hundreds. Priest had liked the place a lot more in the spring, before Sarah started singing here. It left him with a certain ill-defined resentment and jealousy that remained vague but was always there scratching at him.

The jealousy had nothing to do with Septemus. He'd been doing his best to woo Sarah for the better part of the season, and had asked her to marry him about seven or eight times already. He was cordial and respectful of her, gave her lavish gifts, and didn't blackmail or bully her into his bed. He never tried calling in a debt because he'd made her a star in the theater. He didn't often ask Sarah to dinner, and when he did, he made sure he invited Priest along as well. He'd always treated Priest with a curt but affable respect. Septemus knew she had a beau and didn't appear to mind a rival for her love. He still hadn't ordered any of his contractors to try to drop a quarter ton of bricks on Priest's head. Least not yet.

Septemus ruled the Home Hearth well and kept it the kind of establishment they talked about in Virginia City and New York and St. Louis. Europeans frequently showed up alongside Mexican politicians. If any jasper got too far out of his head, Septemus's housemen would escort him out into the alley and not even rough him up. Courtly and cordial, it's how Septemus treated everybody, even Lamarr.

His hands were thick but small, and he clapped for all the entertainers for about half a minute, everybody getting the same amount of applause except Sarah. He gave her an extra few second's worth and usually smiled and nodded to himself, as if he was talking to her.

Griff never smiled, but he clapped for everyone a lot longer, sometimes waving his hat, whistling, really giving it his all. Funny thing for a gunny to do, compromising his hands that way, but Griff liked a good show.

Septemus had to sit up high in his seat so he could see everything. He always got a little nervous with anticipation right before Sarah went on. Priest felt the same way.

He thought about Miss Patty telling him to make some noise so that Sarah would know he was there, but it wasn't like that between them. She'd know it because he'd said he'd be here, and no matter what else had happened between them, he'd never lied to her. Not once, over anything. Besides, with the footlights in her eyes and the orchestra tuning up and the crowd getting even more wild, how was she supposed to make him out in the back of the room, no matter how loud he yelled? He waited, and his chest kept tightening until the curtains fluttered.

Sarah O'Brien walked out on stage.

Even after being featured weekly for the past couple of months, she sauntered forward like this was a vast and unknown terrain. She was a petite woman and took small steps, her slim hips working beneath the dress. She wore a slightly embarrassed grin, cocked to one side. It seemed to take her about five minutes to cover the distance to the center of the stage. The place quieted down, everybody feeling that something different was about to happen.

In one way, Sarah appeared much smaller, standing there surrounded by the proscenium and those thick burgundy curtains. In another fashion, she loomed larger, commanding the theater's attention, her chin held high, her dark eyes full of that Irish glare but no fear.

Every time he saw her like this he wondered how they'd ever fallen in love in the first place, and if it was really over between them or if he could somehow win back what they'd already lost.

Of course, she wore a hat—a wide green bonnet that flapped a bit as she walked. The big bow in front trailed ribbons, and a draft flicked the streamers all over. The curls of her black hair swept out from beneath, framing her face. Her heels made soft thumps against the shining wood. She looked childlike, as if her parents had prompted her with a little push from behind the curtain.

Sarah made eye contact with the conductor in the pit, who threw out his chest and cued the musicians. She began to sing.

The song, like all the songs Septemus chose for her, was banal and immediately forgettable. Though she'd never been to Dublin, her slight brogue—left over from her father—caught hold of the lyrics as if she'd just hit the Americas. In common conversation you could barely notice it unless she was angry, but now as her voice lifted so the back rows could get it all, the Irish came out with real power.

A few of the miners and trail crew bosses were still perplexed—this girl singing had a long dress on, and you couldn't see her knees. Not even her ankles. A beauty for sure, but what, no dancing? Where were the spangles, the tight black stockings? A drunken murmur worked around the crowd, the way it usually did before they settled in to listen.

Priest shut his eyes, trying to block out the trite lyrics and the excessive horns in the pit, the drummer bashing away like crazy and thinking he was the only one making music. He had gusto and flair, but that was about it. Sarah tapped her foot so she could keep the rhythm going in her head. Priest wanted to go over there and kick the damn drum in, tell the dumb bastard to open his ears and not come in pounding on every beat. She was trying hard to hold on.

A pair of violins slipped by clear and clean, underscoring Sarah's tone and inflection perfectly. Her voice, at this moment, gave him the feeling that he was slowly being wrapped in something soft, the same way his father's music had pressed like a cool rag against Priest's fevers when he was a child. Papa would play the fiddle for hours, sometimes half the night long, to help when nothing else would.

His father, Dr. Preach McClaren, didn't know why the music worked when the medicines didn't, but he was thankful for it. He played all the time, even though Priest's mother, Kate, was deaf. She'd rosin his bow, hand it to him, and occasionally lay out sheet music so he could attempt some classical pieces. Sometimes he tried them, but more often he'd just let loose with "Down Yonder Is My Heart" or "Range Fire Winds Blowin'." It didn't get by her. She'd sign that she could feel the vibration so long as Daddy sat beside her, and she'd clap along and tap her heels, usually in the right places. She liked how everyone smiled, singing along. Molly would sit on her lap so that Mama could look at the side of her face and watch her laughing.

Priest could let himself go on in his reverie, wanting and loving Sarah but doubtful they'd ever get back to where they were. Maybe it was better that way. Probably, anyway, for her.

Sarah's brogue swept him along, back to the days when they made love in the shadow of the saguaro. She'd move her hand through his hair, stroking his temples, and say, "My man, my beautiful man, close your eyes. After all that loving work, you've earned yourself some rest now. Don't you worry your head at all, I'll wake you in time for a second go." He'd sleep for an hour and awaken to her squeezing plum juice into his mouth.

Somebody shook him by the shoulder.

"You're in my seat."

Priest kept his eyes shut a moment longer, listening to Sarah on stage, Sarah lying in the copper-colored sand and loving him, his father playing the fiddle and Molly laughing, Mama clapping. The guy shook him again.

"I believe this is my seat."

Priest looked up. "I've been sitting here the whole time."

"I think you're mistaken."

"No, it's true."

"I'll not have any of this. What are you trying to pull?"

"Nothing."

"Here now, let's have none of this nonsense."

Priest enjoyed men like this, sometimes, when he thought about it. Certain confrontations were a blessing, when you got that surge of anger in your belly going quiet for a minute. He stared at the pudgy guy, who had arching high cheekbones, a Colt Peacemaker holstered at his side. Patience was trying for a law that stated no guns inside the city limits, but it wasn't going too well so far. Priest didn't know how the man had managed to sneak the gun into the theater without one of the housemen spotting it. Maybe he slipped by because he just didn't look like he should have one.

"I said you're in my seat, sir."

"But I—"

"I'd appreciate it if you got out of it now. Now, sir."

There wasn't much sharpness in the voice, and only a little fear. He was still being polite, even adding in the "sir," but getting more peevish by the second. The accent made him from Georgia, and wearing the gun into the Home Hearth proved he was new here in Patience, a little too wary, with a need to prove that he'd take no guff off anyone. Heads began turning. Priest thought about getting up and sitting elsewhere just to end this before it became a big play—if the housemen got into it now, wielding ax handles or worse, there'd be even more trouble.

The man put his hand back on Priest's shoulder, not shoving, not squeezing, but showing he had some mass behind him and he'd use it. Priest searched the stranger's eyes, looking for a hint of stealth. If he was from the South he might know Septemus, and Priest still wasn't completely sure Septemus wouldn't set him up one day exactly like this.

He didn't see it, though, and wasn't sure why men like this always wanted to push him, to see how far the bones could go before breaking. The southerner drew his head back like a chicken about to peck. He unbuttoned his coat and started to angle his body sideways so he could draw if he had to.

Priest sighed loudly enough to catch Sarah's attention. She knew that sound and looked shocked to hear it now. She turned in his direction, her voice lifting and aiming straight at him, eyes wide. She made a few fluttery gestures in his direction, hoping he'd get out of the place.

"Oh hell," the man said, turning and squinting into the surrounding rows, finally getting his bearings. "I nearly started a ruckus for no reason atall. I'm the one who's made the mistake here, but you know that already, son. I needed to attend nature's calling and got spun around in the darkness. My eyes are bad. The western sun does them no good in the day, and this desert moon is no help at night. There's my chair over that way, I believe." He held his hand out. "My apologies—you've my word it won't happen again."

Priest looked at his own hand and saw it was empty, surprised he hadn't pulled his knife. He reached over and shook hands with the stranger. "It's all right."

Sarah was still moving her fingers a little as the song came to an end and the southerner wandered back to his seat. Priest noticed Griff staring down at him, and he did his best to ignore the fact. If this had been some kind of play put together by Septemus, Priest couldn't figure out what it had accomplished.

You could see the yahoos enjoying themselves. Sarah sang for nearly an hour in all, and after each song Septemus gave her exactly the same amount of applause, like he was counting off the number of times he clapped, leaning forward in his balcony seat. When she left the stage Priest left too, heading for the dressing rooms. The audience let loose like they always did—even a rowdy crowd of trail crews and cowhands could appreciate talent when they heard it, even if it did keep its clothes on. There were even a few bellows of "Encore!" to be heard, but Sarah never came out a second time.

The orchestra struck up again, and now the drummer's banging was exactly right for the music. A group of dancing girls made their way through the curtains in a kick line and the Home Hearth went berserk. Look at all the knees. The cleavages, plenty of skin and black garters. It was only eleven o'clock, and by one A.M. the theater would empty and Miss Patty's would be packed.

Surprisingly, the stage manager waved him through. Usually he had to remind everybody of who he was and that he had permission to see Sarah, but the housemen gave him a free pass. He kept close to the wall as folks bustled past him, men climbing in the scaffolding, acts rehearsing, and the magician's assistant still looking for a stray magpie. He knocked softly on Sarah's dressing room door and it opened instantly, as if she'd had her hand on the knob.

She lunged for him, coming in low and quick like she was trying to escape the room. His gaze swept the room to make sure there wasn't anybody else in here. It was empty. She moved closer, and for a second he thought they were going to kiss. His muscles loosened, and he got ready to wrap her up in his arms until he realized she was sniffing at him.

So that was it.

Priest controlled himself and kept from sighing, waiting it out while Sarah checked his breath for liquor. She was surprised to find that he wasn't loaded.

"Well, now," she said. "What in the wide world would you be doing back there, Priest McClaren?" She almost sang it at him, angry enough that the brogue came on sweet and strong.

He smiled but knew it made him look drunk, so he quit. "You saw me from the stage?"

"I know the sound of your voice, don't I, now? Who in God's name were you wrassling with while I was doing my best to tame the ruffians?"

"No one, really. Someone who got turned around in the dark. It was a simple mistake."

Priest saw how it affected her, the sudden strain in her face. Her hands tightened on his elbows. "Did he have a gun?"

The hell made her ask that? "Well, yes—"

Her mouth drew into a mottled line. He didn't exactly understand why she was so upset. There'd been little enough trouble in the Home Hearth, and he'd never caused any of it. So had Septemus set him up? And did she know about it?

Sarah's black eyes smoldered, and he could almost let himself ease down into them, the blackness like nothing he'd ever felt before except when he was in her arms. He tried to draw her nearer, but she resisted.

"What's the matter, Sarah?" he asked.

"You're asking me that?"

"Well, yes."

"I saw the flash of light on metal."

"That could've been anything."

"No, right where you stood."

"It must've been from somewhere else."

"I know what I heard, Priest McClaren, and what I saw."

"Calm down, Sarah."

"Don't you be telling me to calm myself. You drew your knife, didn't you?"

"What?" He didn't know how they'd gotten here, or what point she was trying to make. "No, I didn't. Of course not."

"Yes, you did, quick as a snake, waving it about."

"No, I didn't. I checked."

"You checked? You have to check now, do you? You drew it and put it away so quickly you don't even remember doing it. I've seen you do it before—I know how it's done."

The slow creep of cold sweat prickled his scalp. Could that actually have happened? Is that why the stranger had backed down so quickly?

He wanted to touch her face, but the damn hat was in the way. He undid the long ribbon and drew the bonnet off her, letting her hair flow out across his fists. For a second it seemed as if she might let him embrace her, but she did a quick sidestep and slid away.

"You're all the news fit to gossip about this evening, Priest McClaren. I've been hearing words about you from all the riffraff. Tell me now, were you feeling a bit too bored in your settled ways? What'll you be doing when you need attention in the coming days? Burn down Padre Villejo's mission?"

It's not like he didn't expect as much. What caught him off guard was her vehemence. That temper was as much a part of her as her beauty, and despite how often he was the object of her furor, he wouldn't want her any other way. "Listen—"

"And you've left the poor old man in the hands of whores."

"He's used to them."

"Oh yes, of that I'm sure. You may not mind tearing down your own future, but did you have no thought to your own grandfather? With what will you pay his way? Have you enough money saved for even half a pint? Will you urge him back to the reservation to eat the government beef with his Apache mates?"

He moved in again to touch her face, and this time she didn't avoid him. Instead, Sarah held a hand out to stop him where he stood and pressed it hard against the center of his chest. She was petite but had a real strength that could still startle him. "And what of Lamarr? Now that you've finally torched your own store."

"No, see, it was Chicorah, he—"

"I'll not have you splitting whiskers with me. You look as if the heavens themselves have fallen from your shoulders."

He didn't feel that way anymore. The tension had come crawling back into him until it was as bad as ever. That change he'd been hoping for had led to something else, hideous and no real change at all. What happened was that he'd hit the wall hard and now there was no more running. He had to turn and face things.

He said, "You sang beautifully tonight, same as every night."

The glowing black embers dimmed a bit, but she didn't puddle up. He'd seen her cry only once, and he didn't ever want to think about that again.

But at least it brought them a little of the way back. Just a kind word, especially an honest one, right when you needed it, could do it from time to time. He hoped she still loved him a little.

"Flatterer. And your intentions, Priest Mc-Claren?"

When she said his surname like that he thought of angry schoolteachers calling him up before the class. "I don't know," he admitted. "I'm not sure."

He saw the surrender in her after that, in the way she sagged as if she was too tired to continue fighting him. Something bad was coming, and he could only sit tight and wait for it to arrive. She leaned against her dresser, resigning herself to what was about to come. He crossed his arms and did his best to keep from slumping. She said, "Septemus Hart asked me to be his wife this evening."

"What's that, the tenth time?"

She nodded. "As likely a number as any, I suppose. The difference is that this time I'm considering it seriously."

Priest's stomach froze and the hairs on the back of his neck bristled. So this was it. He didn't believe Sarah would ever really consider marrying Septemus, but the fact that she'd say it proved they'd come to another turning point. They stared into each other's face for a long while, but their eyes never quite met.

Every one of his regrets came alive at the same second, especially the child. He could tell she was thinking the same thing, and that made it all the worse. He didn't want his head to go around to it again, but there was no stopping his thoughts.

He grinned, because it started off well and

made him happy. How Priest had once been a daddy for a week.

When Sarah had told him she was pregnant he beamed like a wet-brained fool until the hinges of his jaw hurt. He walked across town with a ferocious smile on his face all day long and found himself laughing out loud everywhere he went, because there was still a chance to make his life work out right.

She dropped weight and dark circles formed around her eyes. She got the chills no matter how many blankets he piled on her, and all he could do was hold her head up while she vomited just about everything she ate. He hadn't learned a damn thing from his father, so he had no idea what might help. He fed her tea and tortillas soaked in honey, which was all she could keep down.

The pain became so bad that Sarah couldn't get out of bed on most days, and lay there shivering and crying with her arms wrapped around her midriff like she was hugging the kid in or urging it out. He knew she was losing the child but didn't want to believe it. Sometimes he still smiled, but not in the same way. This was redemption, and this was a possibility to erase the horror of Yuma Dean and Spider Rafe from his past.

Already it was over, and he was helpless to

make it right. At the end of the week she miscarried, and he held her as she wept and scratched at his arms. There wasn't even a breeze to mark its passing. He wanted to climb up into the cliffs and howl, but each time he started out for the mountains he wound up at Tanratty's Saloon finishing off a bottle of whiskey. He kept thinking of the things that were supposed to be but had never yet happened.

When she'd fall asleep in his arms he would peel back her dress and study the smooth white flesh of her stomach, and press his cheek down to her belly. He stared out the windows and stood guard over an empty house that felt like it would always remain vacant and barren now.

It was, as far as he could gauge, where it began to end for them.

By then the bottle had him pretty good, and Sarah dropped into unbearable silences that would go on for days. The potential of the child hovered between Sarah and Priest like every other failure of their lives.

He'd heard of this happening to other folks, but only now realized the immensity of the loss and what it meant afterward.

"Lamarr is back," she said.

"What?"

"Someone told me Lamarr has finally come back."

"Who?"

"Griff mentioned it."

Griff was always scouting for Lamarr, It gave him something to do when he wasn't standing right next to Septemus waiting for something to happen.

"Aren't you even going to ask me not to marry him, Priest?"

"Don't marry him, Sarah."

"You don't sound very sure of yourself," she said.

"I am."

"No, you're not. But don't you think it's far past high time, Priest McClaren?"

"For what?"

She raised a fist as if she might break his jaw. "For what he asks. Merciful Christ, give me strength." Give them both strength. She glared at him for being so absurdly thick. He felt that way, too, and pondered if it would ever wear off. He wanted to press his face to her belly again, and try again to feel the growing life of their love within her. She saw him staring and knew what it was about. The moment broke, and she said softly, almost like she was singing to him again, "To be certain, Priest."

"Oh."

"To be *sure of something.*"

That was easy enough to answer.

"Yes," he said.

He sure as hell was going to get a drink.

Chapter Six

Priest walked through the batwing doors of Tan-ratty's Saloon. The scarred and splintered mahogany bar had been replaced sometime in the past three months, and the new shining brass rail looked like it was polished every night. Some gambling took place here, but not like in other parts of town. They had two roulette wheels, keno, and a couple of middling-stakes poker tables. No faro, though.

It didn't take him aback any to see Lamarr sitting alone, singing one of the slave songs his mother had taught him before he'd strangled the plantation master. It did surprise Priest a little that none of the furniture had been toppled yet, no bodies on the floor with broken limbs. Coloreds weren't welcome in this part of town, north of Main Street. They weren't welcome south of Main Street either, but they had to stay someplace, and those five or six square blocks behind the livery were considered the black quarter.

Lamarr lived outside of town, though, on hardscrabble land in a solidly put-together shack. He hated Tanratty's but since they had no faro, he could relax without his gambling demon driving him wild to ride the tiger. Relax for as long as he could, until somebody threw a chair at his head or brought in a lynching rope. The only other Negro was a teenage boy who swamped the place out and cleaned the spittoons.

Lamarr looked like he'd been here awhile, all day and night maybe. He upended a bottle of tizwin and finished it in a gulp, which meant he didn't have any money for mescal or whiskey. He was wearing a new bright yellow sombrero.

"Freak strike of lightning?" Lamarr asked.

So he wanted to get into it, right off. "Chicorah thinks we're destined for better things."

Lamarr laughed at that until heads turned around all over the place. "If Apaches knew shit they wouldn't be huddled on the rez starving to death."

"Not all of them are."

"Yeah, but them renegade boys'll be back soon

or the army will just shoot 'em all in the heart. Surprised Chicorah chanced coming all the way into town. He must've felt it was important."

"Where's the goods?"

"Funny you should mention them. I got a very entertaining story to tell you on that subject—"

"It's a two-day ride down to Haloosa Creek."

"Well, yes."

"You've been gone three weeks."

Lamarr cleared his throat and put all he had into his smile. It glowed so white, Priest had to squint to look at it. Even seated, you could tell that Lamarr topped six two and weighed in at around two hundred and thirty pounds of muscle and bone. He had a presence nobody in the same room could avoid. His short hair was fringed with a little white. The red sash he wore around his waist all the time was dirty and faded.

"See, I never actually got to Haloosa Creek. Sadly, our plans went awry."

"Imagine that."

"Now I sense a bit of upset in you, but I swear by the sweet baby Jesus hisself that—"

"Hold on."

Priest bought a bottle of whiskey at the bar with the money that should have gone to buying Sarah a new hat. He didn't think he needed to go to Miss Henshaw the milliner's in the morning anymore; times called for more extreme measures. Lamarr didn't lose the smile, but he eyed the bottle and two glasses closely. When Priest poured himself a drink, Lamarr pushed the tizwin toward him and said, "This might settle your thirst."

"Not even nearly."

"Whiskey'll just give you them dreams again."

"You want to share this bottle, or am I going to have to drink the whole thing by myself?"

Lamarr knew better than to argue. "When you put it like that, I realize there's nothing else I can do but help out my friend by drinking half his bad dreams off for him."

"You're so good to me. Now, where the hell've you been?"

That smile kept shining until Priest had to shift his gaze. Lamarr's eyes drew back into slits as he tried to appear like an inscrutable Oriental but mostly just looked like he'd been kicked in the head by a horse. "Stopped in Tombstone for two days and got to see Fatima at the Bird Cage."

"And that's where you lost most of the money."

"I didn't exactly lose it. I know where it's at."

Lamarr had no interest in poker or roulette or billiards or any other game that cities like Tombstone thrived on—none, except for faro. Something about it fascinated Lamarr, and a divine expression of purity would fill his face as he gave up all his cash trying to buck the tiger.

"The point being that you no longer own it."

"That is an important point. I admit to having dropped a dollar or three at the tables and stretching out Fatima's garter a tad. Then I headed on down to Sonora. I got you a sombrero almost as fine as this one, but I lost it in the river."

"I forgive you dropping the hat so long as you let me borrow that one on occasion."

"Well, I'll have to think about that some."

Priest felt almost afraid filling the tumbler with whiskey. It really hadn't been all that long. He threw back a shot and then had another so fast that he didn't get any of the taste. He'd been missing the slow burn down his throat. "I sat in that empty store every day for three weeks while you been whoring and gambling in Mexico."

"Course, I didn't spend all of it. I bought me this here handsome sombrero, and likewise the one I lost in the river, as already mentioned."

What the hell was it with everybody and their damn hats? "Must have impressed the ladies."

"Well, no, see, I bought it after I already finished impressing the ladies. I deserved a fine gift for that, but them ladies was all too tuckered out to go shopping for me."

Somebody wanted a ruckus and called out

across the room, "Nigger bastard, sitting in here like he owns the place!"

No need to say or do anything about it right now—things would all work out in a few minutes. Priest had another double, and Lamarr said, "Hey, I'm supposed to be drinking half that bottle for you. How about you slow down some?"

"My suggestion to you is to pick up your pace."

"I like to enjoy my whiskey." He took a small sip. "Pleasure like this shouldn't be rushed. But then, you ain't never had any gratification that came out of a bottle."

"I wouldn't exactly say that."

Priest was going to bring up the time they first met, two years back, when Priest was drunk and stumbling in a hog pen and Lamarr needed to talk to somebody about finally finding Septemus Hart, his daddy. Words gathered but didn't want to come up. Priest started to say it, but then wound up letting loose and telling him about dreaming of being tied to his mother again, watching Molly shoot it out with Rafe. He stared into the empty shot glass, wondering why the stuff always made him talk too much.

"Spider Rafe is dead," Lamarr said. "I got to explain this to you again?"

"Not at all. You weren't even there."

"No, but I heard about it plenty. They took eleven bullets out of him."

The mortician had missed one. Molly had unloaded Daddy's Colt .45 pistol into Rafe's chest, and about six minutes later Priest went back inside the house and sat in the chair stained with his mother's blood and emptied his father's Remington Frontier .44 into Rafe lying on the floor. He didn't stink any worse afterward than he had when he was alive. It felt like the man would never be dead enough. After each slug tore into the body, Priest waited for him to grin and get up.

It wasn't until much later that he'd cleaned Rafe's knife and started practicing with it.

"Yuma Dean is still out there, though."

Lamarr said, "Chances are he's long dead, too, the way he went at life."

"Bet Septemus thought the same of you before you showed up on his doorstep calling him Daddy."

"I had a reason to live. Man like Yuma Dean ain't got any."

To hate and to kill and to take another drink or more morphine could be considered plenty of reason. The liquor and drugs focused Dean's life, gave him an incentive to get up in the morning, to rob banks, to take another breath.

"Nigger lover!"

Priest said, "They talking to me or you?"

Lamarr thought about it. "I suppose it could be directed at either one of us."

"Yeah?"

"See, truth be told, I've loved my share of niggers."

"I learn more about you each and every day. Any other secrets you feel like unloading?"

"A couple. Just hold on some and maybe I'll share with you."

Lamarr stood and turned to the group of drunks who weren't going to let it go. For all of Burke's faults, he would've broken this up easy without anybody going to jail, but no one was about to go run and get him. Priest reached for his knife, but it was gone. He looked around and saw it tucked into Lamarr's red sash.

Lots of action in the saloon now, with glass splintering and a card table going over. He saw two or three men piling onto Lamarr, with Lamarr starting to laugh, which still wasn't so bad.

He didn't realize how hard the liquor had hit him until he got to his feet. No wonder Lamarr had been able to grab the blade without his noticing. His brain swirled and he heard his name being called again, this time in a child's voice. Maybe a boy, maybe a girl.

They called him some more names, and a miner with a sheen of dust across his knuckles grabbed Priest by the neck and wrenched him to the left. The child kept getting louder, the words that weren't quite words starting to become something more, but he couldn't tell what. He tasted blood and bile. The miner brought his fist down, aiming for Priest's forehead. It came closer and closer, and just before it hit the voice told him to move and Priest moved.

He dodged the blow and leaped across the table, diving onto two men struggling to grab hold of Lamarr's legs. Priest couldn't cough loose his bitterness and kept gagging and snarling. Noses caved in beneath his fists and he wheeled around, thrusting his elbows up under chins, feeling the jaws give. Men sprawled all over the place, and Priest continued fighting. Lamarr was laughing, so everything was all right.

He kept swinging and connecting, making sure nobody was about to draw. Only two of them had gunbelts and they were both already lying in the sawdust. Priest wondered if the bartender was going to reach down to one of the hidden shelves and bring up a shotgun and break things up. Priest looked but didn't see anybody behind the bar anymore.

The child's voice told him to watch it, but Priest didn't turn fast enough. A blur of black motion appeared above him, and he spun in time to get his arm up high enough to partially block a chair swinging for his head. It clipped him on the temple, and his head exploded with furious colors.

Lamarr stopped laughing.

It had been a hell of a day. Priest's vision kept unfocusing, while Lamarr beat the shit out of the rest of the jaspers, and finally he let himself start to black out. He was sucked down into the silent darkness, and he hoped he wouldn't have the dreams again.

He woke up one time. His face was wet and he didn't know if he was sweating, bleeding, or crying. Lamarr carried him over his shoulder, heading toward the horses.

"How'd we do?" he asked. His tongue was swollen, but it felt like all his teeth were still in the same place.

"Good enough, I reckon. 'Cept I think somebody might be following."

"Let me throw up and I'll be more help."

"You done thrown up everything except your gallbladder, and I figure that'll be next. And you still ain't worth a damn. How about you just go to sleep."

"Okay."

At least the child's voice had stopped. That was something to be grateful for as the murkiness closed over him again.

Lamarr said, "I swear, Honest Abe knew how to hold his liquor a lot better than you. Though he used to get a little weepy, too."

Chapter Seven

Murder blows in the door like prickly pear blossoms on the wind.

His father, Dr. Preach McClaren, had been a man of raucous laughter. His mother, Kate, a silent woman full of cautious grins, who'd lost her hearing at the age of five to scarlet fever.

He remembered the scent filling the house and seeing flower petals waft over his mother's shoes. Looking up, a little higher, watching her skirts drift back and forth. Molly heard the front door handle bump against the back wall, and the sound roused her from the other room, where she sat trying to get her dolls to drink from a cup of cider. She came in carrying the dolls under one arm, the cup in her left hand, with her yellow print dress blazing as rays of sunlight fell on her. "Daddy!"

Then Pa took a step inside, smiling sadly with a knot forming on his forehead and a few drops of blood dappling his collar. Yuma Dean came in next, one arm propping up Spider Rafe and both hands filled with his pistols, two Colt Peacemakers that had dried mud on them. He had saddlebags draped over his shoulder, bulging with rope and sacks of banknotes and documents, but hardly any money. Rafe was nearly unconscious, and when he tried to talk nothing came out but long strands of red-speckled phlegm.

Mother made to move forward, and Pa stopped her with a flick of his hand.

Dean said, "Behave and we just might all get through this alive."

Pa's voice didn't waver, even though there was an eddy of panic in his eyes. "I don't have any of my medical apparatus here. If you'd listened to me, we could have taken him to my office."

"Into the middle of town, carrying a man hacking up his heart's blood? No lawman would've noticed, with ladies screaming? You got your head and hands here at least. We've got knives. You can boil water."

Even back then Priest realized his parents acted with an amazing amount of calm—Molly too. No fear showing, no shouts or tears. He couldn't take his eyes from the bruise turning blacker on his father's forehead, the little trickle of blood flowing across the length of his eyebrow, catching on lashes, and dripping down to the shirt. Molly stood and lingered, blinking frequently but slowly, taking everything in and waiting patiently. One by one the dolls fell, but her knuckles turned white around the cup of cider.

All of Priest's nerves contracted into his left hand, and no matter how hard he tried he couldn't control the awful trembling in his last two fingers.

Spider Rafe stood on his own for a moment while Yuma Dean shut and locked the door, then slammed the shutters on every window in the room but the one facing town. Dean had been careful to take off Spider's guns and stick them into a second belt he had tied around his waist.

Rafe began to stagger sideways and had to prop himself against the kitchen table. The pearl-handled knife sheathed at his waist clattered against the wood. Blood poured down from his torn brown vest and splashed in wide patterns across the floor. He cocked his head to get a better view inside the main bedroom, and stumbled toward the comfort of the canopied bed.

Molly broke in front of him and guarded the doorway. "Don't go in there."

Rafe smiled, showing crimson teeth, and tried to sweep her out of the way. Molly easily dodged aside and took a step closer, holding her ground. Mother hissed, but Molly didn't move.

Yuma Dean had a face made up of angles that didn't seem to meet at any of the right places, soft as clay. His eyes were two black rocks tossed in the dirt. "If you give me any more trouble, I'll kill your daddy."

"You're gonna shoot us all anyway."

"I just might at that."

Mother tried to draw Molly away; Molly sidestepped but reluctantly fell back. Even so, Rafe didn't enter the master bedroom but shuffled to the sofa, sat straight with his hands on his knees as if expecting tea, and passed out sitting up.

Preach McClaren, prisoner in his own home but still a doctor, put water on the stove to boil. Dean eased the pistol around to the side of Pa's head and pressed the barrel hard against his temple. "I'll tell you this now while the water's still cold. You try to pitch a heated pot in my face and your whole family's dead."

Papa said nothing, though his eyes echoed Molly's words. Priest's fingers flapped even worse, and he tried to ball his hand into a fist and grind the fist against his leg, but still his pinkie stuck way out, twitching something awful.

Pa got out his smaller medical bag, the one he

never took to the office, and said, "Move him off the sofa. Lay him flat on the dining table and open some of the shutters—I need the light."

An odd silence dropped. Dean had lost a lot of concern for Spider Rafe, and he moved slowly through the house. He left the shutters closed but found a lamp, lit it, and turned the flame up. New shadows were cast over the room, with the thick blood trail across the floor turning black in the dim light. Dean kept staring at Mother, his gaze roving but always returning to settle on her. His face was full of hatred, lust, and more, maybe shame, probably jealousy, the kind of hardened rancor that a man with nothing felt for everyone else.

"Stop looking at me, you witch."

"My wife is deaf," Pa said.

"Tell her to stare someplace else. I don't like it."

Breathing shallowly, Rafe's gasps kept time with the popping bubbles of the boiling water. Papa carefully cut free the shirt and vest, and Priest plainly saw the splayed muscle and chips of bone in the exit wound near the left side of his upper chest.

Pa had to move Rafe to the table alone as Yuma Dean picked objects off the tables and put them down again. Pa had wrestled the dead-weight three or four steps before Priest finally came back to himself and moved to help.

He didn't hear the click, but found himself staring into the cocked Peacemaker pointed into his face. Dean said, "The hell you doing, boy?

"My father needs help carrying your partner."

"Make sure that's all you do, you twitchy little bastard."

Pa bundled the torn, stained clothes and said, "Molly, these are covered with vermin. Burn them in the fireplace and fetch me blankets, bandages, and a pillow for his head."

Molly didn't move. The cider had spilled out, but she still held the cup. There was a small crack in it now. Papa turned and glared, and she gave it right back. Mother stood and grabbed the clothes, but she didn't know what to do with them until he signed and pointed to the fireplace. She nodded and went to get kindling.

Priest knew Dean would have something insane to say, and waited for it. A few seconds passed, and then a few more. Dean gave a weird bark that sounded like laughter, full of raw malevolence. "You going to send a signal, Doc?"

"A what?"

"A smoke signal."

Papa fell back a step, his disbelief evident, so shocked that he nearly grinned. His jaw cocked slightly to the left as he gnashed his teeth. "You think chimney smoke will alert the marshal? It's a cold evening, so how do you figure anybody will notice?"

Later, Priest would hear talk of how cold and hard and balanced Yuma Dean was supposed to be. About how he fought posses out of box canyons, broke jail twice, raided Mexican villages, and killed war parties of Apaches all alone. Even bloated tales had their truths, but the reality here was something much different. Yuma Dean, on that day, had come apart, and kept looking at Mother.

"Where's the morphine?"

"I don't keep any here in my home."

"Whiskey, then."

"I don't keep—"

"Where is it?"

"I just told you—"

Talk about twitchy, Priest thought, his pinkie doing all kinds of things. Dean swept back to the corner, brooding and savage with the need for liquor and drugs. He was sweating much worse, and the sweat smelled like corn mash.

"Morphine. Give me some."

Father didn't argue anymore, and kept his voice low and easy. "You're drying out. It won't help you in your condition. It'll just make you worse."

"Give it here, damn you!"

"I've already told you, I don't keep anything like that in my own home."

"Goddamn you to hell for lying to me, you son of a bitch."

There were two guns in the house—Papa's Colt .45 and his Remington Frontier .44—but they were both in the main bedroom. The well-oiled Colt was in the back of the closet, and the equally clean Remington was in the top drawer of Pa's bureau. Priest had to get into the room, and he didn't know why his father wasn't trying harder to maneuver inside.

He realized now that Molly had made a mistake, and he'd been wrong in wishing her on. If Rafe had lain down on the bed inside, their father would've been within easy reach of his Remington. He could've made up any reason to get into the drawer—bandages, sulfur, morphine.

Priest thought he could do it. His shaking hand didn't matter right now. If he got into the bedroom and grabbed the gun, he could come out here and shoot this man who'd pistol-whipped his father and terrorized the family.

Pa was already at work on Spider Rafe, probing for the bullet and draining the wound. As the knife went in, Rafe would abruptly open his eyes and gasp, mutter and try to sit up, and then black out. No one would ever be able to eat off the table again.

Dean was in a stare-down with Molly. He stepped forward and crushed her dolls under his boot heels. She didn't seem to notice, and just kept glowering. Priest decided to make an effort. "There are more bandages in—"

"You go sit down," Dean said to Molly.

"I don't want to."

"Don't sass me, you mouthy half-pint pain in the ass."

"I ain't sassing anybody. I just don't want to go sit."

Mother was hunched over the fireplace burning the clothes, occasionally looking back over her shoulder at Papa. She saw what was going on and rushed over to engulf Molly in her skirts. Dean held the pistol on Mother and waved them over to the divan. Molly let herself be dragged backward, the crack in the cup getting bigger.

"I said quit staring at me!"

The front door hadn't been shut all the way, and a draft eased in. The prickly pear petals rolled all at once, spreading out in a widening arc across the broken doll parts and the spatters of blood and cider.

Maybe Papa would help out this move. Priest asked, "Do you need any more bandages, Pa?"

Pa drew the back of his hand over his forehead, wiping the sweat and blood from his eyes. The knot on his head was large and red as a wine sap. He stared at Priest and said, "No, not right now."

"Sit down with them, Twitch," Dean ordered.

"But—"

From Pa now. "Do it, son."

At first Priest hadn't been sure if Papa had any idea what Priest had in mind, but hearing that extra-harsh edge in his voice, he realized his father knew and didn't want Priest to try anything at all. Just sit there beside his mother and sister, the three of them waiting it out while Yuma Dean sneered at Mother and Rafe kept shuddering and hopping awake on the table, blood squirting out of him in tiny, powerful streams.

Dean started going through the cabinets, throwing dishes and glasses aside as he hunted for liquor. Priest watched it happening and clearly saw Dean going further out of his head, losing what little control he had left.

Priest felt an incredible rage burst inside him, aimed not only at the gunmen but at his father too. He figured Pa could have grabbed a pot or flower vase and brained Dean by now, if only he'd get his nose out of Rafe's wound. If Pa wouldn't do anything to help them out, then Priest would have to do it himself.

Just thinking in this manner made him lightheaded for a second as he breathed in the stench of the burning clothes. His trembling fingers began to tug even farther away from the rest of his hand.

But this unexpected fury was soothing, too—he no longer wanted to get the Remington and give it up to his father, but instead wanted it for himself now. He was a fair shot and decided that all he needed to quell the violent nerves was to grasp the butt of the pistol, point and fire, and hold on.

Molly sensed what was going on. She frowned and said, "Daddy, he's leaking something awful all over our kitchen table. I'll get them bandages for you."

"Sit with your mama, girl, and let me do my work." Pa even stared at her for an extra second, making sure she understood him. Molly worked her lips, blinking rapidly, as if she couldn't quite believe he was going to let this go where it was headed.

"Yes, sir."

Did Pa really believe if he fixed up Rafe's chest everything would be all right? They'd just mosey out there with their saddlebags stuffed with stolen banknotes, shake his hand, tip their hats, smile generously, and be out the door?

The house had darkened considerably in the late afternoon, with most of the shutters closed. The leaping, crawling fire threw lithesome shadows across the room. Mother's eyes, which were her main way to express her thoughts and feelings, grew too wide and wild to bear. Even she thought Pa was making a mistake.

Flames reflected and whirled in her eyes, making it seem as if she were weaving in her seat, nodding her head. Dean noticed and kept watch, occasionally giving a nod to her as well, as if he thought she might be telling him things. He was sweating worse than Priest had ever seen a man sweat, and the sour mash stink grew more diseased.

Spider Rafe's hands suddenly came up and he grabbed Pa by the neck, throttling him. Pa gagged and tried to break the grip but couldn't. He coughed and cried out, and eventually Rafe came back to himself, loosened his hold, and sat up. He whispered, "Whiskey."

"None here," Dean told him. "First stop before we get out of this here hell berg is a saloon. Told you we should've hit one for a few drinks before the bank."

"Shut up, and get me a shirt."

The exit wound looked so ugly and raw and lethal that Priest couldn't believe Rafe was still alive, much less sounding strong. Pa was a damn good doctor.

Dean waved the pistol at Priest. "Do it."

Priest got up and stepped into the bedroom, feeling Molly urging him on from behind. He heard the cup finally giving way and shattering to pieces that scattered across the floor. His last two fingers were pulling so painfully that he had to chew back a groan.

He moved to the bureau—the second drawer with Papa's pressed shirts in it, the third with his ties, ironed handkerchiefs, gloves, his watch and watch fob, and the Remington—and put his hand on the brass handles. His fingers rapped so quickly and loudly against the metal that it sounded like he was ringing a bell. Priest yanked his hand away. Dean stood in the doorway.

Priest, with the irrevocable brunt of realization, thought clearly, *This is no longer Pa's fault. It's mine, entirely mine. Whatever happens from here on out is only because of me.*

"The hell you doing, Twitch?"

Priest opened the second drawer and got out one of Pa's nicest shirts. He handed it to Dean, who grabbed Priest by the neck and dragged him out of the bedroom.

Rafe put the shirt on without so much as a moan. "You didn't even think to tie 'em up, Dean?"

"Thought of it."

"Well, get to doing."

"What's the point now?"

"Jest do it."

Dean picked the saddlebags up from where

he'd sat them on the chair. He uncoiled ropes, and papers dropped all over the floor. He was having such trouble drying out that he couldn't see well enough to tie the knots tightly. He kept scowling at Priest, daring him to try something reckless. Priest swallowed a growl.

"Don't go mad dog on me, boy."

Rafe said, "How'm I going to be, Doc?"

"You'll survive," Pa said.

"Pity the same can't be said of you and yours."

Spider Rafe flicked his hand out, the pearl-handled blade like just another part of him, and stabbed it hard into Pa's side. He twisted it once, twice, withdrew the knife, jammed it in again, and pulled it out. Dr. Preach McClaren, who liked to dance while he played the fiddle, shrieked and hopped around, stopping directly in front of Priest, who could only stare in horror with his mouth wide open.

Dean said, "We going to kill them all?"

"Unless you got a better way of hiding our tracks."

"I always hated killing women and girls. You do them two, I'll fix the doc and the boy."

"Sounds fine by me."

Yuma Dean rushed up behind Pa and pressed the barrel of his pistol to Pa's head. There was a second there where Pa appeared to be confused and angry with himself, shaking his head, about to say something to Priest as Dean smirked and pulled the trigger. Priest felt a gushing splash across his shoulders as fragments of bone cut into his neck.

Rafe plunged the knife into Mother's belly. She made the first sound he'd ever heard from her—not quite a grunt, but sort of a low moan like nothing he'd ever heard before in his life. Listening to it made him scream.

Mother pitched forward and flopped free of the loosened rope. Molly didn't even yell, she just snaked free and jumped out of her seat, grasping Priest by his last two flapping fingers. Priest managed to bring his elbow up and catch Rafe under the jaw, knocking him back into Dean's arms.

This was Priest's fault—it was all his fault.

Molly led him into the bedroom, shutting and locking the door. She went for the Colt .45 pistol in the closet while Priest slowly opened the bureau he couldn't open before and finally grabbed the Remington .44. He was right about one thing at least: The second he touched that grip, the tangled nerves in his hand were fine.

The Colt looked gigantic in Molly's tiny hands, but she knew how to hold it the correct way, aiming at the door and getting her footwork right so the kick wouldn't knock her down. The lock on the door exploded as Rafe shot it twice, laughing now like everything else had just been leading up to this game. The door flew open and Spider Rafe stood there in Papa's clean white shirt, no seepage at all from his wound. Priest had the Remington aimed exactly between Rafe's eyes, but Molly beat him to it.

She fired once and flame and blood blossomed low on Rafe's belly, the shirt burning. Rafe staggered backward but didn't fall, just staring down at his belly now like this was just another inconvenience, still smiling a little. Priest stepped toward him.

Spider Rafe aimed his pistol at Priest's chest, the grin thinning into a startled expression. Spider wondered why he was bleeding again, how this could be, when Priest hadn't even pulled the trigger yet. Priest waited for him to figure it out while Molly blew on her bruised hands and set her stance again. Rafe snarled and gritted his teeth, straightening his arm out and raising the gun once more even as the flames burned away at the shirt and curled up toward his beard.

Priest had all his faith in Molly, not worrying as Rafe cocked his gun. Priest took another step forward, grinning a bit himself now. Molly fired a second time, catching Rafe in the knee and spinning him to the floor. He squawked in pain and said, "Jesus Christ, the girl, it's the damn girl. . . ."

Priest walked over to him and kicked in his

chin, feeling the bone crumple beneath his boot. He scanned the rest of the room for Dean. It did him some good to realize Yuma Dean was a coward and had already grabbed the saddlebags stuffed with stolen money and run for it without his partner.

He rushed outside, hearing the Colt blast twice more, and twice more after that as Molly emptied the gun into Rafe. He saw a dust trail and ran to their small corral to saddle up their horse. He stumbled in a red puddle while the horse thrashed on the ground, wheezing with pink foam gushing out its nostrils. Dean had shot it twice in the side.

He watched the dust trail dwindling into the distance, receding along with everything he had ever known before, that bark of laughter floating back toward him.

After he finished killing the horse Priest came back inside, plucking shards of his father's skull out of his neck, sat in the stained seat, reloaded the Remington, and emptied it into Rafe's corpse.

It took him a long time to pick up Spider Rafe's knife and clean his parents' blood off it. But he finally did.

Chapter Eight

They'd tried lynching Lamarr again, this time from a goddamn spruce.

There's pine and birch and ash trees all over, and still they strive to hang him off the side of a spindly spruce.

Priest staggered out from behind the clusters of thorny-stalked ocotillo brush. He brought his hands to his temples, trying to hold his throbbing brains in and not doing too good a job.

He stared at the bodies lying in the dirt and all the scuffs on the rocks, putting it together.

"Christ."

He could just see it going on: these three ranch hands all twisted inside from drinking and losing at faro half the night, no money left to pay the whores for another go-round. Nothing left but the prospect of going home to their indifferent wives or mean ranch bosses without even two coins left between the three of them.

Maybe they were in on the fight earlier or maybe not. It doesn't matter. So they come stumbling outside with sour bellies and they follow Lamarr carrying Priest across his back. They ride the two and a half miles out of town and find Lamarr lying on a boulder outside his shack and wearing a sombrero. This big black buck topping six two, two hundred and thirty pounds, probably still singing. And there on his head is this brand-new bright yellow sombrero.

Funny how so many of them think you could cow a colored man simply by sneering at him and calling him nigger. They get off their horses without even bothering to ground-tie them, mosey on up to him and start in with the insults. Lamarr, being who he is, says something to them like, "My good Lawd Jesus, these peckerwood sumbitches have come to hassle a poor colored man laying on his property in the beautiful dawn. I think I am so shocked that my eyes may never completely close again, so wide are they in amazement and total surprise."

Priest kept checking all the signs, reading the scene in the dirt. This is just about the point when they get the rope and knot it to the goddamn spruce, and Lamarr guffaws for a long while until his ass is ready to shake out of his pants. He holds the sombrero and waves it into his face to get some air.

The horses know what's coming and get skittish, start backing away. The three yahoos don't cotton to no black man laughing at them, so somebody runs to get his rifle out of the saddle boot while another sits on the dead log over there finishing off their last bottle of whiskey. The third one does some rope tricks with his lasso. Hoping to toss it nice and easy over Lamarr's neck, yank him along kind as you can be, oh yes sir, thank you much, and watch him swing.

Lamarr stands there while this idiot tosses the lasso, and Lamarr is beaming and holding his stomach because he's laughing so hard while the rope falls at his feet, brushes his shoulder, goes flying way off in that direction. He puts the sombrero back on and tells the farmhand, "Here now, aim for the tippy-top point. Nice and slow, let it out by the wrist. Come on, now, I know you can handle this sort of pressure we got here."

The guy who went for the rifle finally reaches his horse and starts running back, dragging his boots hard in the dirt and kicking up clots. He slows down to take aim when the lasso finally knocks the sombrero off Lamarr's head. It falls in the dust and spins around before landing right side up.

Lamarr pulls out his converted .36 Navy revolver, which he always keeps at the small of his back stuck in the red sash. Still smiling and showing every wide white tooth off, he fires three or four shots and ends the party.

Priest sighed. It was getting late. Hours had passed but Lamarr was still sitting there on the boulder, the three bodies having been stacked up like cordwood behind the rocks.

"Weren't no cowpokes this time."

"No?" Priest said. "It's what they look like."

"Well, yes, I mean they were, but that's not all."

"What, then?"

"Some of Septemus's men."

Priest sighed again and rubbed his eyes. So maybe this was going to be the final touch that got Septemus's undivided attention.

"Way I figure it, we can do one of two things," Priest said.

"I just hate it when my options are so limited," Lamarr told him. "You sure with all those big thinks of yours you can only come up with an itty-bitty two things we can do?"

"We can ride into town and tell the sheriff what happened . . ."

"Uh-huh."

". . . and you can claim self-defense . . ."

"Uh-huh."

". . . and I can bring you cookies in jail and dig out those nice shiny boots of yours you keep in you closet, just so you look your best when they hang you."

Lamarr whistled and patted his stomach. "I admit before heaven to liking your cookies aplenty."

"Mama taught me how to sew, too. Second course of action being we ride out to Septemus's place and bring him his fellas back and see what kind of play he makes."

"But you ain't promising to make me no cookies, then, if we follow that latter course, now, are you?"

"No, I'm not. Figure there won't be enough time to do any baking, seeing as how we'd have to start out about now before these here boys start stinking the valley up."

"Damn." Lamarr seemed to give it considerable thought. "Well, all right. Guess we might as well go see my rich white daddy, then." He let out a laugh that didn't end for a minute, and by the time it did Priest's chest was layered in sweat and he had chills working up his spine.

Lamarr had been born and grown up on a Georgia plantation owned by a man called Thompson, his mother just fifteen years older than him. His daddy was the plantation master's boyhood friend, both of them having attended West Point and serving in the War with Mexico together. That's all Lamarr knew of the man except his name, which was Septemus Hart. When Septemus made his annual visit to see his friend he liked to bed the prettiest women on the plantation, whether colored or Indian or white. Lamarr figured he had a whole bushel of brothers and sisters on the grounds, but he never tried to find out exactly who was his kin. Only his father mattered.

When Septemus was found in a bath with Thompson's daughter, their long friendship was ended. Septemus had to put some ball shot in Thompson's shoulder just so he could make it out the window without any pants on. Couple years later, when Lamarr strangled Thompson, he sort of thanked his dear old daddy. Thompson couldn't raise that arm much in defense, and Lamarr got to take his time, first choking the master with his left fist, and then his right, making it last a good long while.

It took Lamarr fifteen or twenty years to track Septemus to Patience. By then he'd fought with the Yankees against the South, even though Union officers weren't much better than men like Thompson, when you got right down to it. Still, he'd killed his fair share of Confederates as part of the army, and before he deserted he got a chance to kick his white sergeant's teeth out and leave 'em scattered across Chattanooga.

The killing didn't stop there. On his way west, he'd run into rustlers and dry gulchers and plenty of highwaymen of every stripe, including Mexicans and Indians and a band of ex-slaves who liked to think of themselves as hombres when they set fire to any sod house they could find on the prairie.

Lamarr discovered Septemus here in Patience almost two years ago, living on a hacienda and owning nearly half the valley, and still taking up with every pretty girl he found, the old bastard. Lamarr introduced himself to Septemus by saying, "Why, hello there, Daddy, been a while since you come round visiting your kin. Figured I'd pay you a visit." Lamarr, smiling and giving a nice throaty laugh, maybe raising his eyebrows some, then just walking away. He'd been pressing Septemus every chance he got since.

The first time Priest had met Lamarr he'd heard his entire story. Priest was drunk again, having the screaming fits behind the livery, seeing the ghost of his murdered mother flitting all around him. He'd stumbled into a hog pen and would've been stomped to death if Lamarr hadn't gotten him the hell out of there. Priest not only remembered every detail of Lamarr's story, but he also recalled trying to get up from the dirt and clean some of the hog shit off him, with Lamarr just standing there and repeatedly shoving him back down in the mud while the tale went on and on. Priest knew the whole account now, except the ending, of course. He couldn't eat pork anymore, either.

Priest draped the bodies over Lamarr's pack mule, then got back on his sorrel. "You could always just kill him, you know."

"Wouldn't be no fun in that."

"You been nipping at him for two years. Must be getting a tad boring."

"I admit he ain't reacted quite the way I was hoping for," Lamarr said.

"Which is?"

"I'd settle for apoplectic."

"He's too refined for that."

"Didn't seem too refined the day I saw him running without his pants on across the tobacco fields." He eyed the corpses, wondering where they were going to lead him. "After we drop these three stinking boys off on his front step, maybe he'll be a bit more riled."

"If you want him to draw on you, all you have to do is challenge him," Priest said. "He's never backed down yet."

"When's the last time you seen him do a thing like that?"

"Quite a while ago. Not many folks duel in the middle of the street anymore, especially considering the amount of horse flop we got piling up now."

"Still a few, though."

"Yep."

"Even Molly."

"She doesn't give most of them a chance to draw. None of this clomping down the street with your spurs jangling, staring each other down till the clock strikes noon. Most of them are drunk and laugh in her face and try to feel her up some first."

"Figure this is a more private matter than shootin' it out on Main Street with all the women folks and children about, standing in horseshit."

"I figure it the same way. Just don't expect him to hold still while you throttle him."

"Sure hope not."

They rode out to Septemus's hacienda, Lamarr wearing his yellow sombrero the entire way there across the foothills. Even from a quarter mile off you could make out the ornate wrought-iron gate that stood closed before the ranch. A couple of sentries spotted them and ran to the corral to saddle some horses, but they never did ride out. Sweat puddled down into the small of Priest's back, but Lamarr looked like he was almost sleeping in all the shade that sombrero threw.

They drew up to the gate and Cobb, the foreman of the ranch crew, stood on the other side, glaring, with a little smirk tugging his lips out of shape. He eyed the dead men on the mule and started chewing the inside of his cheek. Cobb's hands didn't stray to his gunbelt, and Lamarr just kept smiling, not touching the Winchester in the saddle boot close to his fist. Flies swarmed the corpses, and the stink was getting worse. Priest didn't exactly like Cobb, but he saw no reason for the man to die, either.

The moment drew out. Cobb decided to be smart and relaxed his shoulders. He ignored Lamarr for the time being and said, "McClaren, you have any hand in this?"

"No," Priest said. It sounded a bit cowardly, like he didn't intend to back Lamarr's play when it came to that. Best to make his intentions known right from the start so nobody would be confused when the time came around. "But they were after some killing, and that's what they got."

"You side with this nigger buck son of a bitch and you'll be making the worst mistake of your sorry stupid life."

"I appreciate the kind words of advice, Cobb."

"Just listen, you—"

"But the truth of the matter is that I'm partial to that there sombrero and I don't want to see it

107

come to any more harm. I'm planning on borrowing it for the spring dance."

Lamarr perked up. "Borrow this here fine sombrero that resides upon my head at this very second?"

"Yep. You said I could, seeing as how you lost mine in the river."

"I said I'd have to think about it some, and I'm still contemplating on it. What makes you think I might readily turn over this hat to you?"

"Well," Priest said. "I was meaning to broach the subject with you a little later on."

"Broach it now. This I'd like to hear, about how you plan to wear my sombrero and sweat it up with all that long hair of yours. That's why I bought you your own."

"The one at the bottom of the river. See, that dance is next week, and I was figuring on asking Sarah O'Brien to it and—"

"Sarah O'Brien?" Lamarr frowned and shook his head. "She's too much woman for you."

"I beg to differ on that account."

Seething, Cobb made a guttural sound and growled at Priest, "Why'd I expect a yellow-belly like you to listen to reason? What with your dead mama in the ground five years and you never even going after the man who done it. She'd spit in your eye, you drunken—"

Priest pulled and hurled the knife in one fluid

motion, winging it sidearm almost absently, so that the blade sort of glided straight-on. The pommel struck Cobb in the chin and knocked him backward on his ass. Chips of his bottom teeth dribbled into his beard stubble, but there wasn't any blood. Cobb moaned, shakily got to his feet, and started to clear his Walker Colt from its holster.

Showing off his own perfect white teeth, smiling even wider, Lamarr yanked his rifle from the saddle boot, gripped the lever and swung it in one hand, cocking it, and let the stock smash Cobb in the chin again. Now there was blood, and plenty of it. Cobb went into a coughing fit, gesturing wildly, while other ranch hands appeared around him. Lamarr held the rifle on them and said, "I'd like to see my daddy now. How's about somebody let us into this damn place?"

They rode toward the hacienda, Cobb groaning while a couple of others fell in beside him and helped him to walk. Others ran ahead to tell Septemus what had happened. Priest stopped and picked up his knife. He saw other vaqueros working the rancheria and wondered when Septemus had started hiring on Mexicans. Five men escorted them toward the main house of the ranch. Priest knew Septemus had given orders about Lamarr, but he had no idea what they might be. It was lucky that the three dead hands were new—if they'd been on long enough to have made friends here, things wouldn't have gone as smoothly as they had up to this point.

Caballero music drifted from beyond a few of the outer adobe buildings. Lamarr sort of shook in his saddle like he was dancing along. They were led farther to the center of Hart's headquarters, to a building Priest had never seen the likes of before—it took him a minute to realize this was a smaller replica of the Home Hearth Theater.

The aroma of broiling steaks and cooked pork rose over them. Priest's stomach hitched to the left. Women's laughter and a lot of voices, singing and carousing. Sounded like Septemus was throwing a hell of a party.

Priest said, "Lots of new faces working the hacienda now. We might want to rethink this some."

"Today's his birthday," Lamarr told him.

"What? And you knew that already?"

"Course. I got a present I'm just itching to give him."

Priest knew Lamarr had been looking for the right kind of maneuver to get Septemus to acknowledge him, but throwing three dead men at his feet on his birthday in front of a house full of guests might be going a little too far.

But Lamarr cut the pack mule loose and said to the hands and vaqueros, "Here, take these men to town. Tell Doc Laidlaw the mortician to bury 'em for me. He owes me a favor and it'll be paid off with this. You understand? I'm the one doing this, not Septemus."

Nobody much liked taking orders from a colored intruder, but Lamarr wasn't smiling so much now and he had a hard tone of authority. What'd they care who paid the mortician or who didn't? He sounded too much like Septemus to argue.

Priest and Lamarr dismounted at the entrance to the private theater and walked in, covered by even more of Septemus's men, who ringed the place. Priest was surprised so many people could fit in here. Must've been all of a hundred folks having a good time down on the floor and sitting up there in the tiers of seats. He recognized a lot of faces but didn't expect to see so many Mexican officials and their families eating and drinking and dancing, with tiny kids running around holding candy and toys. So Septemus was making business deals across the border as well.

He was also somewhat puzzled to see that Sarah wasn't here. Either she hadn't been invited or she'd spurned the invitation.

And there he was, the man who owned it all, seated at a table near the stage with a pretty Mex girl on his lap, and Griff the left-handed gunny stationed in the same spot as always.

Septemus stood maybe five eight in his boots, with the firelight glinting off all his brass buttons and medals and the sheath of his Confederate saber. Lamarr had no trouble with walking right up to him, wearing the yellow sombrero, and grinning, waiting patiently.

"What the hell are you doing here?" Septemus asked without the slightest trace of anger. He was actually chuckling.

"I never could resist a big ole grand party like this."

"Should've tried harder."

"Maybe," Lamarr said.

"Heard you took down some of my men."

"Yep."

"I should string you up for that."

"Attempting to string me up is what got them boys in trouble in the first place."

Griff slipped up behind Priest and said, "Shall I escort these two off your land, Mr. Hart?" Septemus ignored him. Griff leaned in close and whispered, "One of those men was my cousin."

"You should've watched over him better," Priest said.

"When I settle the score with that Lamarr, I'll make sure to save you some."

Priest had known men who weren't worth a

damn at threatening, but he figured Griff was about the worst at it. "Umm, well, I appreciate that, Griff. I certainly do."

"You won't be laughing much longer."

"Okay."

Septemus, though, kept chuckling. The air was starting to thicken with tension. "You haven't told me what the hell you want yet."

"I wanted to have a drink with you on your birthday," Lamarr said.

Septemus had as many teeth in his head as Lamarr did, and they were all just as big and white. He never dropped the smile for a second, and everything he said had that chortle running through it. "I don't drink with lice-riddled niggers."

"Funny that. Ma said you shared plenty of bottles of whiskey with her, getting her drunk when she was only a child so she'd bed with you. And you never complained once about bedbugs 'neath her sheets."

The snickering came on strong then. "Your mama was nothing but a black pig who hardly ever got out of her bed. She liked laying with her masters—don't you think any different."

Priest didn't think anything could rattle Lamarr. He'd just taken care of three men trying to lynch him and none of it had come close to getting under his thick hide. So it was twice as big a shock seeing Lamarr's face tighten up until he didn't look like himself anymore, that big fist slowly rising into the air, swinging out to backhand little Septemus out of his seat and onto the stage.

Priest said, "Oh shit."

Nearly every gun in the place must've been pulled at once, so that all you heard was one loud slap of leather and a hundred hammers and levers cocking. The Mexican Federales had plenty of soldiers along with them to protect their families. Priest figured there was no reason for him to draw his own pistol, so he just stood there forcing himself to breathe.

Septemus rolled for a while, four or five times over and over, until he finally came to a stop. When he did he just sat there and shook his head and laughed some more.

Lamarr undid his gunbelt, let it drop at his feet, and stepped out onto the stage, the sombrero still high on his head. He'd gotten his calm back but looked a bit guilty that he'd lost it in the first place. Septemus let out a yelping guffaw, stood up, and drew his saber.

"Why, Daddy," Lamarr said, "I admit I'm mighty impressed by the length of your sword."

Septemus might've been short, but he was solid muscle packed with energy and controlled anger. You didn't build, own, and keep half a city unless you regularly fought for it and always won.

He swung the saber wide, slashing high, expecting Lamarr to dodge low to the left. Lamarr did exactly that, and Septemus was already in position, waiting with the flat of the sword, when Lamarr's face showed up in the right place. The pommel crunched against Lamarr's nose, and he made a wet growling sound while the blood ran down the back of his throat.

Septemus made a bad mistake, though, just standing there watching and enjoying the sight, expecting the blow to stagger Lamarr. It didn't even slow him. Those fingers came closer. Lamarr had a lot to reach out for—the coat sleeves, the lapels, the epaulets—and his giant fist seized on Septemus's collar and hiked him high into the air. Septemus attempted to stab now, no longer playing games, but by the time he tried to thrust down into Lamarr's throat, Lamarr had already punched him clear across the stage again. Septemus rolled some more as Lamarr stomped closer. He kicked out and caught Septemus in the ribs.

The theater was completely silent, even the children. Everyone watched, but only a few of the guns had been put away. Priest kept his arms crossed, away from his pistol and knife. Septemus's orders about Lamarr must've been that if the man ever showed up looking for a fight, let Septemus alone with him.

Stabbing out again, Septemus sliced upward, the blade weaving and landing on Lamarr here and there. Grunting in pain, Lamarr backed off fast. He was suddenly cut in five or six places, the wounds fairly shallow, but leaving him bleeding all over.

Septemus got up smiling and laughing. Priest realized it was all true in that second, Septemus Hart really was Lamarr's daddy, and the old man knew it and even liked Lamarr a little for coming after him.

As long as Lamarr didn't kill him, they had a chance of getting out of this alive yet.

Dancing forward, Septemus thrust the blade into Lamarr's shoulder. It went in a full inch. Lamarr let out something just shy of a scream, a cry that was only partly pain. The rest was roiling hate and rage for all that had gone on beneath the composed exterior his entire life. He struggled forward even as the saber twisted in his flesh. Septemus withdrew the blade and tried again.

But Lamarr had had enough. He caught Septemus's wrist and bent it back until the sword went flying. His fist snatched out and clamped onto Septemus's throat and held him up, way up in the air, while Lamarr took his time beating the hell out of the old man. His fist reared back and came driving in again and again, smashing his daddy's face wide open. Septemus didn't give in easily, though, and before he fell he got one good blow in himself that rocked Lamarr back and knocked the sombrero soaring.

Griff had drawn his gun and stood there just waiting for the chance to use it. Priest figured he could cut his throat pretty easily, but some of the Mexicans were bound to get splashed, and that wouldn't do any good in making friends.

The sombrero was still tumbling, and it rolled over to Priest's foot. He picked it up and held it like a prize. He had to gain some height and do this quickly. In two swift steps he hopped up onto the table, kicked Griff in the face, jumped down, and punched him in the jaw. Griff's eyes came unfocused, but he was still trying to aim. Priest slapped the sombrero onto Griff's head so hard that he felt the gunny's nose wedge in there nice and snug.

Priest aimed for the bulge and smashed Griff backward into the first tier of seats. The second he did he knew that here it was, there's no backing out, one of us has to die now—if not today, then soon.

"You done ruined my hat!" Lamarr cried.

"I apologize for making a mess. I know how close you were to it. But it's still fine."

Septemus crawled to his feet and staggered to his chair, huffing hard, with blood running from both nostrils and both corners of his mouth. He dropped back some and licked his lips. He grabbed the whiskey bottle and drank—and drank some more, like he wasn't ever going to come up for air. When he finally finished, he had tears running down his cheeks.

He shoved the bottle across the table to Lamarr. It was still about half full. Lamarr filled his lungs, upended the bottle into his mouth, and didn't stop until the last of the whiskey was gone.

By the time they got back to the shack, the liquor and loss of blood had caught up to Lamarr and he was too drunk and tired to move much. He just lay there on the bed, smiling. Priest figured Septemus was probably doing the same, for different reasons.

He hoped that the one drink would hold them both over for a while, at least until the next time father and son decided to have a family reunion, maybe tomorrow or next week, when things were bound to end differently.

Chapter Nine

A rim of sunlight sprinkled gold across the ashes of the store. Priest stopped off at Sarah's house first, but she wasn't at home. She wasn't at the milliner's, either. A nervous unease he hadn't felt while packing three dead men across a horse began to slither through his belly and back muscles.

It was early enough in the evening that most of the girls at Miss Patty's place were still asleep. Patty, Wainwright, Fat Jim, and Gramps sat in the parlor, drinking coffee and talking. The men were laughing loudly, and Patty just smiled easily. This was a family scene—perhaps his family, but probably not.

Priest stood in the hallway a minute, watching them in that mirror up in the high corner, feeling like an outsider. The heat followed him inside. Patty tittered now, joining in, and that same jab of the past came in high. Fat Jim lit a cigar, and Gramps pulled out his pipe and borrowed the flame.

Only Wainwright spotted him there, those steady gray eyes catching him in the mirror the second he had opened the door. Gramps said something low as he let out his first hiss of smoke. Fat Jim burst out laughing so hard that his derby rolled off his head, and Patty had to slap him on the back a couple of times.

The hell was so funny?

Gramps was white again, a failed farmer and onetime railroad man who could tell a pretty good story about his years working with the survey crews dynamiting through mountains, always watching for pockets of methane. If you asked him about Chicorah or what he'd been doing the past six weeks living with the Apaches, he wouldn't know what you were talking about.

Gramps wore suspenders and a bow tie, and sat there with his knees crossed, blowing on the coffee. He looked like a literature professor just passing through Patience on his way to a huge university in the Northeast. Priest felt a twinge of sentiment shake through him, remembering when his grandfather used to take him fishing and explain some of the wonders of the world to him. He wanted to talk to the old man but didn't know what to say. Gramps was grounded right now, and Priest didn't want to do anything that might rattle him loose again.

He stepped inside and barely made a ripple in the ambience of the room. Patty brushed her fingers across the seat beside her, and he moved toward her. Gramps turned in his chair and smiled warmly. "Hello, son."

"How are you feeling, Gramps?"

"A mite better than you, I daresay. You been brawling again?"

"A bit."

"Then I know it was for the honest reasons and with good intent."

"Yessir."

"A cornered man can't help it sometimes. Have some coffee with a couple taps of whiskey in it—help you feel better."

"He doesn't take whiskey anymore," Patty said.

Priest told her, "Pour it."

He never quite knew how to react when Gramps was lucid. They could hold a fine conversation right now and catch up on lost time, but by the end of the week the old man might not recognize him anymore. It made these moments tenuous, special, and almost unbearably important.

"We heard you had a touch of trouble over at Tanratty's last night," Patty said. With all the traffic coming in and out of the house, Patty was the most informed person in the entire town.

"Wasn't much," Priest said. "Compared to what followed this morning."

Nobody asked what that might be, waiting to see if Priest went into it. Patty poured him some coffee with an ounce of rye in it, and he sipped like the rest of them. The silence continued. Fat Jim tilted his head, puffing the cigar, settled in for a tale. Wainwright looked at him expectantly.

Priest felt a sliver of guilt that Gramps had stopped talking. He needed to hear a story that might get him laughing so hard that somebody had to slap him on the back. Patty crossed her legs, one knee bobbing toward him, that white ankle slipping out from beneath her skirt to tempt him. He glanced at her thighs. He wanted to make love to her out in the open someplace, down in the grass where it was cool and shady. More than that, he wanted her to quit staring at him, this silence unrolling way too far, getting out of hand now.

"You just aren't happy unless somebody is trying to bust your head," Patty said, with some of the same sanctimonious bite from last night. "You smashed up a whole saloon. They're still working on fixing the windows. And what happened this morning?"

"Lamarr had to show three idiots with a rope the error of their ways."

"Oh."

Fat Jim leaned forward and wiped tobacco juice away with the back of his hand. "Did they see the light?"

"Briefly."

Cigar and pipe smoke had a different texture in the air, one swirling clockwise and the other hanging there like a sheet before Gramps's face. Fat Jim wore a weird grin, imagining how it had happened, but also somewhat shocked. "Lamarr in jail?"

"No."

A bit more cautiously, easing up in his seat. "The sheriff clear him, then?"

"Hell no."

Wainwright came in with the firm voice of reason, as usual. The coffee cup was nearly hidden in his massive hand, but Priest could see a small chip in it, and thought of Molly holding the cracked cup of cider. Wainwright noticed and opened his hand, as if to show Priest there was nothing inside it to be afraid of. "If you're hiding him, the consequences will be serious ones for you too."

Even Fat Jim frowned at that one. "Well, of

course they'd be—you don't need to tell the man that. He ain't hiding Lamarr. He wouldn't do nothin' stupid like that, getting involved with that sort of thing." The way he said it showed how much Fat Jim believed that was exactly what Priest was doing.

"No consequences along those lines yet," Priest told them. "The three jaspers were new hands hired by Septemus."

"That's going to rankle him some," Wainwright said.

"Actually not. Today's his birthday, and Lamarr had a nice tall drink with him this afternoon."

"You mean Septemus Hart finally owned up to being a proud papa?"

"Not quite. There was sort of a sword fight, and Lamarr laid him out in front of about a hundred guests, most of them Federales."

"Federales?" Wainwright's eyes got a little wider while he thought on that, the animal always lurking in him ready to burst through. "Septemus cares as little for Mexicans as he does for Apaches, blacks, and the Union."

"He's getting a lot friendlier."

Fat Jim said, "We wasn't invited to the party? You know how many times I seen his naked white ass creeping around upstairs just hee-hawing hisself raw? And that gunny scaring off customers too, standing around glowering at everybody? And we can't get so much as a tap of bourbon or a slice a apple pie from him. No matter which way you ponder it, that just ain't right."

Patty leaned her head back against the cushion of her chair, let out a groan, and took a quick look around the room as if this might be the last time she'd ever see it. Septemus held the mortgage on Miss Patty's house.

"Anything else happen?" she asked.

"Oh yeah. I kicked Griff in the face and knocked him out."

It was an admission to a death oath, and all of them knew it.

Somebody let out a low whistle. Priest checked all their faces, but he couldn't tell who was doing it. The house was stirring, and girls could be heard above, washing and dressing. The sound went on and on, and finally he realized Gramps had his lips pursed, letting the whistle out beneath his pipe smoke.

Gramps stood and started for the door. He motioned for Priest to join him. The whiskey nightmares had given Priest all kinds of flashes, and here was another one. Gramps doing this exact same thing to him as a boy, taking him down to the fishing hole, giving him his first sip of warm beer, and telling him about women and love. Heading back home to freshly baked pie, Grandma in the kitchen with Mother, the both of them with flour up to their elbows and surrounded by batches of cut apples, and Pa coming in late, leaning against the counter, just watching.

When Priest glanced up again, Gramps was already out the front door. "How's he been?"

Patty gazed at the side of Priest's face, a little stunned and frightened that he had a gunny on his tail now. She might regard him harshly at times, but at least she still cared. Griff had killed fourteen or fifteen men in the past few years with that left-handed crossways draw of his.

It took a while, but eventually she let out a hollow, floating laugh and said, "Your granddad's been randy. Got up early, ate a huge breakfast and a bigger lunch, even woke Erin and took a couple turns with her. After she got over being surly from waking up so early, she seemed to get along with him just fine. From the sounds of it, I'd say they both enjoyed themselves."

Priest couldn't keep from cringing. He just wanted to know if the old man had been hallucinating or weeping uncontrollably. There'd been times he wouldn't come out from underneath the bed for a couple of days.

Hearing more than that about his own overly

eager grandpa could pretty much foul a man's day.

Wainwright said, "I've never spoken at length with your grandfather before, even though I've had plenty of chances. Now I wish he'd come around more and I paid more attention to him. He's got a variety of interesting stories left to tell. It bothers me I never understood that before. He's quite an intelligent man."

Priest knew it was true, that it was only when Gramps was in transition from white to Indian and back again that the old man really went out of his head. Clearly, the feral quality in Wainwright had a kinship with Gramps's wild nature. Both of them, excessively civilized for the present, could relate in the need for going savage.

"Funny as all hell," Fat Jim said. "You ever hear the one where—"

"Yes," Priest said.

"—and the sodkickers from Tallahassee come up to him asking for a new shiny dime and instead of watching their mules they decide to—"

Priest remembered them all. "Yes."

Somewhere in the distance somebody strummed a banjo three or four times, then quit. There was a far-off echo that could have been blasting caps or thunder. Priest finished the coffee off and wanted more whiskey. Fat Jim gave a puzzled grimace. "You sound angry, and you didn't so

much as say more than a handful of words to
him. Don't you like your own granddaddy much,
Priest McClaren?"

Again with the name. Everybody always
throwing his full name around when they were
in the mood to pass judgment. "What kind of
question is that?"

"A fair one, I'd venture."

Wainwright shifted in his chair so he could
leap up if he had to. Priest stood, and Fat Jim
sort of sat up very straight, hoping he hadn't
pushed too hard, tobacco juice easing down his
chin. Wainwright tried to break the moment and
said, "Jim, there's a reason why we don't let you
come out from behind the ivories more often."

"I was just askin', is all I was doing."

"My point exactly."

There was no way for Priest to explain his feelings to somebody who hadn't lived with Gramps
or a man like Gramps. There was resentment and
pride as well, and the curious fact of going from
being cared for to suddenly needing to carry the
crazy old coot up the stairs of a whorehouse in
the middle of the night. Gramps had run a few
months with a couple of renegade Apaches, giving the Army a hard time in the north. The old
man had two bullet scars in his ass, for Christ's
sake, that nobody else knew about.

Fat Jim drew on the cigar, the tip glowing a

gleaming red, sitting there anticipating an answer as if he really deserved one. Priest wanted to pick the tiny piano player up and toss him on his ear. He wanted to tell them how much he loved his grandfather, but he couldn't raise so much as a mumble. The sheet of Gramps's pipe smoke still hung in the air like a veil about to descend. Patty touched his shoulder, a sign of tenderness and understanding, and he nearly jumped out of his skin. She'd known Gramps from childhood and through all his numerous phases, happy times and heartbreak. The hell with it.

"He didn't mean anything by that comment, Priest," Patty said. "His mouth is steel-dust quick, but his brain is a burro."

"Me?" Fat Jim said.

"You."

"Me? What'd I do?"

It made no difference. Priest followed Gramps out the door and found him sitting on the porch steps of Miss Patty's, watching the buckboards, chuck wagons, and coaches kick up dust as they moved in every direction across town. Gramps seemed to be in control of himself, maybe too much so, just taking in the pleasant afternoon with no mention of grandmother or Chicorah or Chief Sondeyka, no memory of cringing under the trough.

129

He wanted to hug the old man but didn't know what kind of reaction he might get. The need almost overpowered Priest for a second, hoping to hang on to what was left of his family for a while longer, before everyone completely vanished.

"I ain't been much good to you these past few years, I know," Gramps said. "I aim to change that if I can—and if you'll let me. I want you to understand how sorry I am. It don't do you much, but there it is."

Priest felt as if Septemus had just gashed him in the chest with his sword. He couldn't quite catch his breath after that. "Jesus." Were they really going to have a conversation? Could Gramps hold on for that long? He couldn't recall the last time they'd truly spoken together.

"I heard about the fire at your store," Gramps said.

The old man had been there. "No, see, it was—"

"There was a reason for it. You got the *Ga'ns* spirits in you, son, same as me. It ain't nothing to be ashamed of."

Priest sighed, thinking, okay, so it was going to be like this instead. "Gramps, maybe we should—"

"It's the blood that calls them to lay inside you."

"Blood?"

Nodding now, thoughtful and strangely enlightened in his own way, Gramps drew on his pipe. "The sorrow and venom mixed in your blood. That's the power which calls to them."

"If that were true, every swamper, jailbird, drunk, and peckerwood on both sides of the Rockies would be stuffed with Sondeyka's mountain spirits."

Gramps turned slowly, still puffing, and took a long minute to give his grandson a look of sympathy that nearly made Priest get up and run back inside the house and throw the lock.

"A lot of them are. So full of anguish and fury, getting the shit kicked out of them half their lives, doing the kicking for the rest. The thing that's different is you got real virtue."

"Gramps, I've got to tell you. I'm not that virtuous, believe me."

"You're on the right side of the magic, and that's what counts."

Maybe. Priest decided that he liked his grandfather a hell of a lot more when the old man was either grunting in Apache on horseback or huddled under a bed crying for grandma. This new side to him, the great thinker, had come on too swiftly, dropping out of nowhere after all these years.

"By God, I'm sorry for not being here enough

for you and Molly, but I've been doing my best."

"I know that."

"Don't hold it against me, son. It takes a lot of time to learn how to cinch the spirits and put them to use. I ain't been sitting on my ass like it might appear sometimes. I'm putting all I got into it. Muscle, soul, and life."

It sounded honest, anyway. Priest wanted to ask Gramps if he'd learned anything helpful up there on White Mountain, if Sondeyka and the other chiefs still had any wisdom left after being corralled onto the rez, starved, and froze.

"I'm going to do better by you, I promise," Gramps told him. "That sounds like cow flop, but I'm telling the truth. You won't believe me, but someday soon I'll be there for you when you need me."

"I believe you," Priest said, and was startled to realize he actually meant it.

"Rain's comin'."

Another roll and rush of distant thunder. The sky began to darken and roil. Silver, starlight, and shadow twined together. Priest heard his name again from far off and thought, *God damn it, I'm going over the edge a lot faster than the old man did.* What kind of an Indian was he going to make, anyway? He heard his name once more and saw that it was Burke shouting from down the block, coming toward them at a fast pace.

Sheriff Burke wore another freshly pressed brown suit, the tie still perfectly centered under his collar. He'd spent some extra time this morning working on the mustache. It continued to lean too far to the left, but not nearly as bad as yesterday. He said, "Heard you and Lamarr Russell tore up Tanratty's pretty good last night."

Priest wondered when Patience would grow large enough that everybody in town wouldn't always know his business. "Only because it was necessary."

"I did some checking and found out the men you were tussling with are some new hands hired out on Septemus Hart's hacienda. Considering how little he likes the two of you, you might want to look over your shoulders the next few days."

"Always good advice."

"For you and that Lamarr Russell it is, anyways. The next time they're around, step off the boardwalk, all right? Keep clear of that kind of action for a while, and tell Lamarr to do the same. I don't need any more problems—I've got more than I can handle. I've had to hire on four new deputies to keep up with the rise in theft and fighting and general mayhem since this town started to spread. The Indians are causing all kinds of havoc on the rez now, too, claiming their women are being hassled. Raped. Whole mountain is likely to come down on us soon."

If Septemus hadn't already sent a rider back to town alerting Burke to the troubles, then there wasn't going to be any kind of inquiry. Priest didn't know how to feel about that. Three men were dead. Three redneck peckerwood assholes killed in the name of self-defense, it was true, but still men. Priest knew they meant nothing to Septemus Hart and that the bodies had already been dumped at the bottom of some arroyo ten or twenty miles south of the hacienda.

Mayor Frederick Murdock and his wife, Susan, walked up along the boardwalk looking up at the sky. Only now did Priest realize that even Freddy hadn't been at Septemus's party. The mayor might only be a vacuous political front man for Septemus, but he still should have been invited out for a cut of steak.

What else might Septemus have been hiding with his new friends? And now that Priest and Lamarr had crashed the party, to what lengths would Septemus and the Mexicans go to cover up that fact?

This might be even worse than he'd thought. Priest wanted to get back to Lamarr's shack and check on him.

Freddy appraised Gramps and gave his typically vapid smile. "It's good to see you again, Mr. McClaren."

"You too, Mayor." Gramps stood and gave a gentlemanly bow to Susan. "Mrs. Murdock."

Susan's face screwed into an expression of horror, and she stepped back in revulsion as if Gramps had running sores and had tried to kiss her. Priest had seen this plenty of times before, where Gramps's reputation caught up with him more when he was in his head than when he was out of it. Last night she had barely noticed him under the trough in his breechcloth, whimpering. You could take a cowering madman lightly, but to have him standing here before you wearing a bow tie and suspenders was obscene.

"How's your farm doing, Mr. McClaren?" Freddy asked.

"Haven't had one for about eight years now."

"Oh yes, I see. Very good."

"What is?"

"Yes?"

"What is very good, Mayor?"

"Yes, yes."

Burke looked like he wanted to throw Freddy down a well and scoop Susan Murdock in his arms before the splash. Susan kept nibbling her lip, part by way of flirting with Burke and the other because she was so genuinely disgusted to be in the presence of Gramps. She couldn't take her eyes off him, and kept a keen watch as if at any second he might leap up and give the attack signal to hidden Apaches on every rooftop. Priest couldn't much blame her.

Burke stared at the front window of Miss Patty's house, willing her to step out the door and come join him. He wouldn't be happy until Patty and Susan stood side by side, where he could size them up against each other once and for all and make a decision on where his wasted efforts should go. Susan was trying to have some fun, slowly licking her lips with the tip of her tongue, but Gramps being in the vicinity tended to throw her off. Finally she couldn't take it any longer.

Priest felt the same way, just listening to Freddy constantly saying "Yes" over absolutely nothing, nodding to Gramps, and Gramps nodding back. Burke rocked on the balls of his feet, Gramps blowing thin streams of smoke that hung in front of all their faces.

Susan said, "He shouldn't be allowed to walk the streets."

Freddy blinked into the sun. "Please, Susan, let's not—"

"Really, Frederick, we've spoken on this too often already. You know as well as I do how awful it is to have such a sick man loping along in our lovely city. He should be put away somewhere, for his own good as well as that of our neighbors."

"Loping?" Priest said.

Gramps stood calmly smoking his pipe, his face turned away as if this conversation didn't concern or interest him. Burke knew better than to let it go on. He gritted his teeth and watched Priest's hands, as if Priest might actually go for his knife, make a big scene in the middle of the road by waving it around and threatening to cut up a woman. Susan's beauty and sashaying ass could make a preacher toss his collar in the dirt, but her squeaking judgments didn't set well with anyone.

"Well, how long is this charade to go on?"

"Please, dear, let's start for home before it rains."

"Who knows how many financiers and investors have kept clear of Patience because of him and his likes?"

"Dear—"

"Drunkards and the deranged sleeping in every back alley and hog pen? Isn't it enough that we're here before an established house of ill repute and that the number of saloons in our city has tripled in the past six months alone? The moral values of Patience are dissolving before our very eyes and you refuse to take a stand on any of these important issues. The wonderful new development of this city cannot be under-mined by the likes of these criminals, gutter-snipes, and lunatics."

Gramps looked something like a financier himself at the moment, assessing the situation with a grim smile. He looked very much like Priest's father.

A couple of fellows hovered nearby, wanting to get inside Miss Patty's house but unsure as to what the sheriff and mayor were doing blocking the door. Susan was still going on, and her voice had taken on the quality of one long, persistent buzz that was starting to make Priest's teeth ache. He didn't know where she was in her rant and didn't care. He moved out of the way so the fellows could sneak by and said, "Jesus, that's enough."

"Well, really! Of course you'd say that, being what you are! Indeed you would!"

Freddy couldn't do much else besides say, "Yes, yes," while his wife made all kinds of dis-gruntled comments and jeers. Burke got himself caught in the middle, still hoping to take her to bed one of these days or at least get an agreeable word out of her. He stiffened and set his lips. It threw his mustache off until it leaned as awk-wardly as it had the day before, like some furred creature clinging to a crumbling cliff face, caught in a mud slide.

Freddy said, "We'll be off now, gentlemen. Pleasant evening."

"Good night, Mayor," Gramps said, and gave the same little bow. "Susan."

"Really!"

"Yes'm, really. Night."

As always, Burke didn't know what his next move should be as Susan threw her hips out in a wide arc and she and Freddy walked off. Her twitching ass made the bottom of her dress snap. Miss Patty's house was open now, and he didn't want to be seen going inside during working hours. He was itching to follow Susan as well, send Freddy off on some fool's errand, swagger up behind her, and use Gramps as a topic of conversation that would allow him to finally get the deed done.

He stood in the middle of the street glancing back and forth between Susan's ass and the front porch of Miss Patty's, trying to decide where he had the better chance. His boots popped dust up as he jittered in the same spot until a chuck wagon nearly ran him down. Burke picked his hat up out of the mud, felt up his mustache some more, and wandered off half bewildered.

"Oh, almost forgot," Gramps said, drawing a folded piece of paper from his back pocket. "Telegram came in for us this morning. Messenger brought it over."

"For us?"

"Well, we're both Priest McClaren. For one or the other, I suppose."

The storm circled overhead. Priest unfolded the paper. There was a slight water stain on it, as if Gramps had held it for too long in his sweaty hand, or shed a few tears while reading it.

The telegram read: *Noon tomorrow. Molly*.

Chapter Ten

She wanted to make sure he was on hand and sober. He'd seen his sister only five times in as many years, each meeting lasting only a few minutes, once almost a full half hour. She'd hand over a saddlebag stuffed with bounty money, and that's how he and Gramps got by.

He knew he was a great disappointment to Molly, that he hadn't let the anguish fuel him in the same way it did her. Each of the five times she'd managed to draw herself back to Patience, he'd been so drunk that he hardly remembered what was said. Priest thought he might have held her once, maybe twice, hugging her petite hard body to him and hanging on until his knees gave out. His own sister seemed to be just another part of the same dragging vague dream. He remembered the smooth barrel of a Smith & Wesson American .44 gently sweeping back and forth across the nape of his neck, and couldn't figure out why she hadn't pulled the trigger.

Now Molly was coming home and she was going to stay for a while.

Priest suddenly felt a great urgency to see Sarah, except it wasn't so sudden—the pressure had been growing all morning until his heart was now kicking against his ribs. He tried her house again and she still wasn't at home. He didn't want to press his already strained luck any further, but he realized that he had to go to the Home Hearth to find her.

Thistles swept over his boots. He could smell the sourness of his own sweat as the breeze picked up and layered crisp waves of air around him. The stink of himself overpowered Priest for a moment, so that he stood in front of Hasseler's General Store holding his breath, trying to beat back the pulse of his own past. It didn't work, it never did, but at least he didn't have to smell himself for a minute there. Priest let his lungs fill again and stood gasping, heading for the Home Hearth.

The impulse to talk with Sarah grew stronger until he was running. He hit the door to the theater and saw that his hand was quivering. He still didn't know why. What could he prove to her by bursting in like this? Nothing that needed to be done had even been approached yet. Was he set to marry her? A half hour ago he'd been searching out Patty's thighs and hoping to lay her again. What the hell was he going to say? It didn't matter. He walked inside with his mind completely clear. If Griff was here, then one of them would have to die.

He'd kill to see her—that's how bad it had gotten. It had something to do with the baby, with either the one they'd lost or the one that Molly was carrying.

Sarah wasn't on stage. Priest checked for Septemus's seat of honor in the balcony, expecting him to be there, tending his loose teeth with sherry. The theater was empty, but he heard her voice coming from somewhere, echoing off the distant walls and immense ceiling. That lilt of brogue hung in the rafters and fluttered down to the floor. She sounded extremely close to him, as if she were bending over with her mouth only inches from his ear. He couldn't help it—he leaned toward the song, awaiting the touch of her tongue, and below her voice was the voice of the child telling him to get out now or there'd probably be trouble.

The child in harmony with Sarah, both calling for his attention. He kept turning as if they were working their way behind him, just out of eye-shot. He needed to see Sarah, and with the need came a desperate kind of panic. But he still hadn't reached for the knife, which surprised him. He moved down the aisle until he came to the short set of stairs that led to stage left, where her song was apparently coming from. Magpie shit dappled the steps, wads of dyed feathers clinging together in the tight corners.

He whispered her name, hoping the acoustics would work both ways, leading his words to her. "Sarah? Sarah, I need to talk to you."

Slipping behind the heavy drapes that framed the proscenium, Priest found himself backstage. He'd never seen it before and was amazed at the sheer size of the space. This was unfamiliar ground where everything appeared odd and ill-defined. Ropes, sandbags, set designs, and broad sheets of metal to rattle when you wanted there to be a sound of thunder. The magician's over-sized cards, some costumes hanging and others stacked on the floor alongside fixtures and levers, poles and hooks. Hats all over the place, of course, hats everywhere he looked.

"Sarah?"

Her song came to an end, and the high note reverberated and continued to tremble in the shadows. She laughed, a brief and melancholic titter, and he wondered why, making his way toward her and tripping on boxes of fabric, wood blocks, and paint. When he heard another door open he knew she'd gone out the back way, and he was alone now with the voice of the child telling him that the song had never been meant for him to hear in the first place.

The panic dissipated, but Priest rushed on, looking for the back exit. All he saw were more clown suits and push brooms, backdrops and piles of sawdust. He was going to lose her forever, he was certain, if he didn't find her right now.

Finally he spotted the door and hit it on a dead run, landing him out on Center Street in a drizzling rain. He looked in all directions and even jogged down a couple of nearby alleyways, but Sarah was gone.

Maybe Gramps's *Ga'ns* spirits had decided to toy with Priest some more, flitting around and buzzing his ears. He threw his head back and let the rain wash his face for a minute. He shook his hair out and walked a few blocks until he came to a saloon called the Red Sunset that hadn't been there two weeks earlier. They had a faro dealer who was so luscious that she had the players giggling when she dealt a hand, the curve of her upper arm leading juicily into the swell of her breast as she swept the chips and money off the table.

Priest asked for a beer and two ounces of rye, but the liquor sat in front of him for twenty minutes. The diminutive bartender had flat pointed features and thin lips, and when he came around again it was like being sniffed at by a coyote. "Costs the same whether you decide to partake or not. You got a wife callin' you home then you better git. No reason to take up room at the bar if you ain't a drinkin' man."

"You're right." Priest threw back the shot and beer without tasting either and ordered the same again.

"I'm Sam. If you can do that steady, then you're welcome here."

After Priest finished the rye, he realized how much he never wanted to be drunk again. He'd made the decision before and was curious to learn whether this was a part of that sense of change that had been chasing him around for two days now.

Lamarr's presence forced its way on Priest even before he'd looked up from his empty glass and turned around. The intensity and energy residing in that immense body forced its way across the saloon, and you could almost follow it with your eyes. Chins lifted at the tables, the faro dealer glanced up and misdealt the hand. Those brilliant teeth, always shining like that, could drag people out of bed from around the block.

"You ought to be napping in view of the morning you had," Priest said.

"Never quite managed to nod off. Kep' laughing myself awake again." If possible, his smile had grown even wider and more dazzling than before. Amazing what a punch to your daddy's jaw could do for a man.

"Some of them wounds were pretty deep."

"Naw, nothing I can't shake off." To prove his point he stretched, and the bad shoulder had barely any hitch to it. "Figured we could head on down to the mission and ask the padre what he knows about Septemus's guests, if anything."

"I've got nothing better to do."

"Considering how few things there are in this world you can count on, I feel blessed you're always available."

He wasn't looking forward to the ride. It was twelve miles to the mission, in the rain, past many of the spots where Priest had learned about love in the mud, and where Gramps had been shot in the ass. The sisters had cared for the old man even while giving classes to the orphans and Indians. Gramps had laid on a hastily made litter at the back of the room—still Apache at the time—as the nuns wrote out English words on the blackboard, and the children and Gramps repeated them, learning the language.

"Padre Villejo hasn't left the mission in nine

years," Priest said, "but it's as good a place to start as any, I suppose."

"Those are my exact same feelings."

Sam the bartender slid up and pawed his jaw. Anxiety flattened his coyote features even more. Priest and Lamarr always sat at the corner of the bar where the bartender most likely had his shotgun hidden below. Sam's eyes were wide, and he kept trying to sneak a few feet to his left, crouching sort of but not wanting to look as if he was.

"This is Sam," Priest said.

Lamarr reared himself even higher at the rail so that his shadow fell on the bartender like thirty pounds of mortar. "Howdy!"

"We don't serve niggers."

"That right?"

"It is."

"Well, soon as I see one I'll be sure to let him know."

"Now listen, you lousy—"

"As enthralled as I might be at the grace you're currently showing, easing on down to where that shotgun's hid, I would *sincerely* appreciate it if you'd keep those baby fingers a' yours up here within shaking distance."

"Enthralled?" Priest asked.

"I'se enthralled, all right. Never know when I might want to reach out and take the hand of a man who don't allow no niggers in his place."

"No niggers, Injuns, or Mex's, them's the rules," the frowning bartender said, trying to put a little bite into it and not doing too well.

"Lookee here, dog-puss, you picked yourself an awfully strange place to open a saloon, then. Why, just look in front of you. This boy here's granddaddy is an Apache."

"Sometimes," Priest admitted.

A lot of apprehension surged around the room now, so that Lamarr had to smile at everybody and nod a bit, tipping his sombrero at the ladies.

Sam obviously had a high regard for his own speed. He was going to go for the shotgun any second now, and even if Lamarr didn't draw on him and only punched him in the face, the bartender was so tiny the blow would surely kill him. "Why don't you just oblige me before I put a hole in that natty head a yours."

"Ain't had gnats in my hair since I quit pickin' cotton and tobacco."

Priest gave up on the idea of never wanting to be drunk again and wished he had more rye. He propelled himself forward, bent over the other side of the bar, and made a grab for the weapon. He was shocked when there wasn't one. It took him a second to find a streamlined Smith & Wesson pocket .32 hidden behind several half-filled bottles.

Sam made fists and jumped up and down,

screeching, "Gimme back my pistol, you hear!"

"The hell?" Lamarr said. "Call that a pistol? How long you been in business here, dog-puss?"

"Almost a week!"

"And you're still alive?" Lamarr shook his head and glanced heavenward. "My, my, sweet Jesus surely is considerate of fools."

Priest handed the .32 back to Sam. "If you want to live out the rest of the month, you'll get yourself a cut-down Remington ten-gauge, and don't go hiding it way in the back behind all the liquor. Keep it close, and remember that you can't aim a scattergun, you can only point it. Practice with it some so you can handle the kick."

Holding the pistol with two fingers, Sam didn't know what to do now. He had rules to keep and nobody would back down, so he scanned the rest of the place looking for help. The rest of the patrons had gone back to drinking and talking and gambling. Men at the other end of the bar tapped their empty mugs impatiently. He had to get back to work.

Sam's eyes jiggled a bit in their sockets as he thought about the damage a 10-gauge—or, better yet, a 12-gauge—would do to a fast-talking big black and his slippery wiseass partner. When his gaze got around back to Lamarr, the smile nearly bowled Sam over. "Thanks for learning me."

"Sure," Priest told him, and he and Lamarr, still beaming, backed out of the Red Sunset and into the rain.

"Hope his mama has another son," Lamarr said at the hitching post, " 'cause that there imbecile's not long for this joyful world."

"How about if you leave me at least one place standing where I can get a beer in the future?"

It perturbed Lamarr, the quality of service you got nowadays. "Honest Abe would never have dreamed of drinkin' in such a low-class establishment as that."

"Bet he would have rather been in there than at Ford's Theater."

"Well, yes."

The storm continued to pull together, growing worse by the time they got halfway out of town. Black veins in the clouds knotted and tightened, rain coming down softly at first, but a lot of it. Lamarr despised the heavy wetness and charge in the air, said it reminded him too much of Georgia. He hated everything that reminded him of Georgia except for his mother's slave songs.

Lamarr hummed to himself as they rode through the washes and dry streambeds, past the ironwood shrubs and smoke trees, along the canyon mouth leading to the mission. Soon they passed the high outcropping of sandstone where Gramps had taken lead in his tail while running with the renegades. When they got to the river, Lamarr put both hands on top of his head to hold down the sombrero. "Ain't about to lose me this one too."

"Don't think I've forgotten that you dropped my souvenir."

"I'll make it up to you someday."

"You could start by paying me back some of the goods money."

"I'm afraid that Fatima ain't going to be letting loose her garter belt anytime before long, but as soon as she does, I promise I'm gonna be asking her about them dollars."

Lightning seared the coming twilight, erupting and playing across the deepening sky. The rain came and went, showering in bursts and then stopping abruptly as if a tap had been turned off. When they were kids, he and Molly used to lie out on the back porch and watch the frayed night go to shreds. Mother enjoyed the view too, sitting in her rocking chair and rapping the armrest with her nails when she wanted their attention.

Priest's breathing grew ragged as a familiar sense of enormous sorrow visited once more, as he thought about how often his sister must've slept beneath skies like these, swept over in her bedroll by waves of mud and snow, bitterly cold with nothing but her vengeance to help pass the time. He'd done so wrong by her.

"You're straying," Lamarr said.

Jarred back into himself, Priest got the horse on the trail again. "Molly's coming in tomorrow."

"Yeah? I can see why you might become lost in thought, then. I'd like to meet her." Lamarr sounded strangely sincere, hanging on his words so that something intensely meaningful came through, like with his mama's songs. "Any woman that good at what she does deserves a drink on me. On you, too."

"What she does is kill men."

"But not what you'd call *indiscriminately*, that right?"

"She hasn't so far, anyway. So long as you're not on any Wanted posters, I figure you're safe enough."

There was still enough light coming through the tattered clouds to see how Lamarr sort of went pale around the dark edges. "Umm . . . well, there was a few incidents I ain't exactly told you about, back east a ways. She ain't traveled all that very far, I don't suppose?"

"And I'd suppose she has. Your face decorating any sheriff's office walls?"

"Might be one or two featuring my fine looks."

"I can try to put in a word for you—"

"I'd appreciate that."

"—but I can't make any promises."

"Might be that I'll visit Sonora again," Lamarr said, staring south, "just for a few days."

"Hope you fetch a nice hefty reward price. It'd be one way to pay me back the goods money."

"I'm tellin' you now, soon as Fatima and her garter—"

More sheet lightning rippled and flickered, breaking against the underside of the night, showing up everywhere at once as they came over the last ridge. The church wasn't old, but the mud and stone that went into its walls was, and you could feel the weight of history and penitence standing on your shoulders. They ground-tied their horses and stepped into the doorway, removed their hats, and hung back, watching. There was a funeral going on.

The pews were filled to creaking with people, mostly elderly women in black shawls drawn shoulder to shoulder, who wore their anguish proudly. They didn't gesticulate or rock in their seats. They wept quietly, lining the long pews and occasionally patting one another's dry, wrinkled hands. Men and youngsters appeared here and there, steadfast with flitting eyes.

Padre Villejo stood in the pulpit, slumping heavily to one side on his crutches. He looked like he'd gotten no sleep the last couple of days and had spent his time in a screaming match with God. A worn Bible sat open before him on the altar, but he only stared down at the page with unblinking eyes, swaying a little. Priest started feeling uncomfortable, like when he was a kid with too much starch in his collar and cuffs, just waiting for something to happen.

The dead man in the coffin appeared to still be in the middle of dying. A rictus might have tilted the corners of his mouth a bit, but it was clear he'd been going after whoever had killed him right to his last breath. The corpse had small yellow teeth, and thick white high-brushed hair like Stonewall Jackson's. He'd been brutalized, his cheeks black and sunken from where the bone had been shattered. He'd been dead a couple of days and wasn't going to hold out much longer, no matter what they did with the body. Flowers wreathed his shirt and had been stuffed deep into the coffin with him.

Marks had been sunken into the gray skin the size of rifle butts. He'd died cussing, his mouth remaining open, his upper lip drawn back, framing his final word. No mortician would ever have been able to wipe that expression off his murdered face. If Priest went out that way, he hoped the same could be said of him.

"Old Mex woman got no choice but to wear black her whole later years," Lamarr whispered. "Kind of life is that for a free people?" He was right. By the time she hit middle age she'd be in eternal mourning for someone—her dead husband or sons or grandsons, one falling and then another and another, with all the goddamn guerrilla wars and revolutions going on in the hills every day. To mourn for half your life wrapped up tight inside your own death shroud, crosses on every wall, alone with heartache and the tortured face of Christ peering down. He thought about the waste of such penance, and of where he was headed.

Thunder rattled the roof, the wind kicking up, but it had stopped raining. Echoes hurtled among the mountains in time with the thrum of the vibrating stained-glass windows. An incessant trickle of water came down from the rafters, splashing to the left of Lamarr's boot. Padre Villejo glanced up and took it slow in Spanish, greeting everyone. His voice began as a murmur, almost like a prayer or lullaby, so soothing that some of the children nodded in the pews.

He stood six feet tall on his one leg and crutches. The other had been cut off when he was a child after his father had complained about the village taxes. Sister Teresa and Sister Lorraina sat on either side of him, heads bowed. They constantly checked to make sure he didn't get himself into such a state that he knocked himself over like he occasionally did.

He flipped pages of the Bible forward and

back, searching for but unable to find certain passages. It got him hot. He slammed the book shut fiercely, and the nuns winced at the harsh sound. Padre Villejo started working himself up. His Spanish came out hard and clipped, and the sides of his fists squeaked along the polished pulpit.

"He's afire tonight," Lamarr said. "Must've liked the old boy in the casket."

"I wonder who he was."

"We'll have to find out."

Padre Villejo had a well-trimmed mustache and goatee, razor-thin and intensely brown like the rest of him. The rosary beads tied around his waist ended in a weighty wooden cross that swung around him whenever he gestured, which he did a lot. Everybody was awake now, sitting up straight, faces filled with a real fear. Priest wished he could understand more than fragments of slowly spoken Spanish.

Wild wrath grew. Padre Villejo had a mean God in his eyes now, one you had to serve, cherish, and love all the more for the pain He wrought, but one you could still get pissed off at when the need arose. The more dust you ate, the more blessed you were. He'd embraced a life of quiet sacrifice and loss, but he could rail and brawl when the furor got his blood up. Padre

Villejo could accept God's assault, but not any man's.

Priest had once seen him use his crutches to puncture the liver of a teenage boy who carried a bullwhip and wanted to live the life of a bandito. The kid stuck his hand inside the poor box and stole a few pennies and a candleholder, laughed like a braying ass, and whipped the altar, sending wine and wafers all over the place. Priest watched while Padre Villejo laid the bandito to a thorough waste with those crutches, stomping him first with one and then the other, always jabbing him in the soft spots of the belly, the kidneys, the groin. It took ten minutes for the nuns to pull the padre off the kid, who was crying and vomiting by then, holding the whip out in both hands like an offering, and spewing blood across the candleholder with six or seven pesos ringing him on the floor. Yeah, the padre could get hot.

Sister Theresa was becoming frightened. She didn't like what he was saying and wanted it to end with a hymn, something to get them all back into good graces. Padre Villejo's wooden cross whipped around and nearly struck the nun in her chin. One crutch fell and Sister Lorraina retrieved it, anxiously trying to set it under his arm again, but he wouldn't take it back.

"Think the old boy is his daddy?" Lamarr asked.

"Could be."

"He's scaring the shit out of these old ladies."

"Me, too, actually. He gets a little carried away on occasion."

"He's gonna throw a lick at Sister Lorraina if she keeps jamming that crutch at him."

Certain phrases came out clearly: ". . . this land becomes a place of snakes . . ." and ". . . . such an indignity cannot keep rooted in our bones." Priest couldn't imagine what context they ought to be taken in, and wondered if the rest of the sermon was just as disjointed. The dead man must be a relative—anyone else's murder would not have unsettled the padre like this.

But at the height of his rage and frenzy. Padre Villejo stopped in midsentence, drained of his venom. He stood sweating with tears in his beard, about to topple over, and finally accepted his crutch from the nuns. Water pulsed against the windows as the rain began once more. Sister Theresa whimpered softly and watched the flailing cross slowly come to a stop on the padre's waist.

Four men hefted the coffin and carted it out the side entrance of the church, followed by the silent, mostly terrified mourners carrying candles and lanterns.

Lamarr stared after them, scowling. "The hell they doing?"

"I think they're going to bury him."

"Now? At night in a downpour? He's been stinkin' for two days under all them flowers. Waiting till morning ain't gonna hurt nobody."

"Guess they feel differently on the matter."

"Never did understand the Mexes."

"And you're not ever likely to."

A few of the elderly were too ill to stand out in the rain, and waited in the pews, shuddering and coughing. As the others filed out around him, Priest walked up to Padre Villejo. He stayed far enough away so that a swung crutch wouldn't catch him in the neck. No telling what the man might do when this kind of fever was on him. Lamarr must've thought the same thing, 'cause he kept behind Priest, letting him feel out the situation and take a poke in the liver if need be.

"Padre?" Priest said. Then again, more firmly, trying to break him out of this black haze. "Padre. Look at me."

Padre Villejo didn't glance up, and his voice sounded like something small scratching in the dirt. "I have no time to talk. I must bury a friend."

"I won't hold you up. Lamarr and I will help."

"That is kind of you, but unnecessary." Sister Theresa hovered for a second and let out a long whisper, like a draft fluttering by. Padre Villejo barely let his gaze brush Lamarr. "You are bleeding. You are dripping blood on the floor." Lamarr was good at binding wounds, but he'd probably been a little too dizzy to have done too proper a job of it today. "Sister Theresa will salt and rebandage your injuries."

"Thank her for me, but I ain't been salted since Georgia and don't plan on ever having it done to me again."

"As you wish."

They stood there for a minute in silence. Padre Villejo understood that they wouldn't be bothering him at a time like this unless it was something important. He reached down and grabbed hold of his cross, holding it close to the side of his leg the way a man might hide a gun close to his body before he drew.

"Who was he?" Priest asked.

"That was my uncle, Don Carlos Herrera Villejo. He owned one of the largest haciendas in North Mexico. He bought land here to the west of us and planned to move his home and his herd. He began with great hopes and many friends. Along the trail they were set upon by night riders. Several of the men were killed, the cattle stolen."

"Did you go to the law?"

"There is no law here, *Preste*. Soon they will round up all of us and put our children with the Indians on some mountain. One day we must fight to keep off a reservation."

"Have you been threatened?"

"We are always threatened. This does not worry me. We endure. I only pray that we can remain dignified."

Priest could tell Lamarr wanted to ask why they were holding the funeral at night. He stood in the doorway like a kid getting antsy, watching them digging in the mud with the children still throwing clusters of posies into the coffin, some of the old ladies moaning now to underscore the wailing of the wind. Their lamps kept going out, and the women had to hold their shawls wrapped tightly around them to protect the meager candle flames.

Priest had never seen the padre so defeated, and he wanted to slap some life back into him. Trouble was, Padre Villejo might come so far back that he'd break Priest's ribs. He said, "Tell me more about your uncle."

"He had many friends and many enemies in the government. The army was supposed to investigate the matter. We have had his body out for two days, and visitors have already paid their respects. Two *hijo de putas*, however, tried to mar his face with their pocketknives. I was forced to mar their own faces some."

"Can't say I blame you none for that," Lamarr said from the door.

"I christened many of his sons and daughters.

He helped to erect this church, with his money and with his strong back. He has been waiting three days—he can wait a little longer. What do you wish of me?"

"I think we already got it," Priest said. Lamarr nodded and let out a tiny breath that came from way down in the center of his chest.

"I will ask you to explain it to me someday, *Preste*, but not now."

"We'll help you with the grave."

"No, three of his sons are outside. They have earned the right to bury their father."

An old woman drew herself out of the pew, coughing up half her lungs. She wandered up to Priest and touched the side of his face. He didn't mind. She pulled aside his collar, staring, her skin like dried leaves swarming against his throat. *"Un sacerdote?"*

She had picked up on the padre, calling him by his name, and now she was asking if he was a priest. *"No, abuela, yo no."*

"Implorar por nosotros."

He would pray for them. *"Yo lo hare."* She left him.

"I must go," Padre Villejo said, crutching his way quickly out the door into the thunder, his rosary whirling.

"Pretty big funeral," Lamarr said.

163

"Same day Septemus throws a pretty big party. A fluke?"

"Even Satan hisself would doubt it."

"Septemus rustling cattle now? Not exactly his style, but where that little man is concerned, I suspect anything is possible."

Lamarr scuffled with it some more, imagining his daddy riding out at night with a pillowcase or gunnysack over his head with circles cut out for the eyes. Maybe in the South. "No. More'n likely he just bought the stolen beef. That's the way he'd handle it. He learned somethin' gettin' caught with his pants down."

"And took on the rustlers as extra hands?"

"All them vaqueros at the rancheria."

It was starting to make sense. "That would explain why Griff hasn't made a move yet. He's been busy today keeping all the new men in line."

"And that little confederate paid off some officials and Federales when they got to his door. Nice birthday present for him. Got hisself quite the growing ranch, like an army camp. With all the expansion of Patience, he must feel like he's starting to lose hold some."

"And meanwhile," Priest said, "Sondeyka's people starve because the U.S. government won't even give them enough beef. Burke said the Apache women are being hassled. Raped."

"Kind of thing some rowdy new hands might

do. Shouldn't be the sort of thing that surprises us."

"Still does, though."

"I know. Ain't that somethin'?"

It was. Priest realized with a sudden clarity that this wasn't really a sense of change that had been plaguing him, but an impression of relevance and connection. All the fractured pieces of his life abruptly coming together again.

"We should maybe stay at Patty's tonight."

"I'm afraid I'm a bit too short on cash for that. You think maybe she'd extend me some credit?"

"She'd extend her fist into your face first, and I'm not talking about having fun."

Lamarr sighed and put his sombrero on as they slipped back into the waiting storm. "You're the only man I ever met who wouldn't want to have fun in a whorehouse."

Chapter Eleven

The stage pulled into the depot about noon. The driver and shotgun rider leaped down to the street and looked around the station with expressions of slight amazement. They hadn't been through Patience in a year or so and were shocked by the size. This wasn't supposed to be a boomtown, but it grew like one.

It took both men to unload the trunks strapped to the back of the coach. Priest recognized the smell of gun oil immediately. Good thing he'd brought the buckboard.

He didn't know why, but he wished Lamarr were here.

Priest had thought he might have to take an ax handle to Lamarr to keep him from coming to the depot to meet Molly. Lamarr had hardly talked about anything else last night, even while the girls at Miss Patty's heaped more attention on him than they should've given to someone without money. His very presence scared half the customers off the front porch. A couple of Septemus's new vaqueros stuck their heads in the front door to see if the house was safe for them. Lamarr sat in with Fat Jim at the piano and sang "The Girl I Left Behind Me" and "Come Where My Love Lies Dreaming."

It was bad. Wild dogs in the street went berserk, and a red-faced jasper wearing only his britches came running downstairs to see who was being killed. Nobody was about to tell Lamarr to shut up, though, especially not after Wainwright joined in and somebody else started playing a banjo.

By the time the moon set, Lamarr's injuries and the events of the past two days had caught up with him. He sat dazed and grinning, showing no teeth at all, and Franny led him up to bed. Gramps was sleeping in the room next door, probably with Erin again. Priest hadn't seen her all night long. He tried not to think on it much.

At nine in the morning, everyone in the house was still asleep except Priest and Patty. He'd had nightmares again, but no screaming fits. The memories came on and he could not defend himself.

For about six weeks after Molly had shot Spider Rafe, she and Priest stayed with Gramps in his one-room shack. Pa had tried buying him a bigger place, but Gramps had always said no. So she slept on the bed, and Gramps, who hadn't quite started going out of his head yet, preferred lying curled on some blankets on the floor. Priest didn't sleep much at all, and it took at least one bottle of whiskey to dull his thoughts down from the inferno they'd become, and at least another bottle before he blacked out.

From what people told him, he never totally keeled over. Instead, he spent the nights doing such unseemly things as crying naked on rooftops with his clothes hanging on weathervanes and flinging gouts of mud around in various hog pens. A year or two later, when Gramps started going Apache, folks pretty much figured the McClarens had some diseased blood in their line. Odd that Preach McClaren had been the town doctor, and such a damn good one.

For those six weeks Molly spent her time learning to become a boy. She hacked off her hair with Pa's ax and took to wearing Priest's old clothes. Priest bought her boots but hardly remembered doing it, sitting there in the store with dried pig slop on his neck and dropping a wad of money on the counter without seeing how much it was. Her bust hadn't started to develop yet, and she easily passed for an intolerably angry adolescent boy.

She got into fistfights with kids shooting marbles, searching out bullies just to see how she stacked up against them. While a few could outwrestle her, and she had her nose bloodied a couple times, none of the boys had the same wildness to claw and bite and pull blocks of firewood from a woodpile and smack the hell out of somebody for no reason at all.

She practiced with Pa's Colt .45 pistol and the Remington Frontier .44. Priest woke up one time in the middle of a sentence and stooped outside a tent. He didn't know what he'd been saying or doing. Molly had to prompt him a little. He'd been showing her how to tie a bedroll and make camp.

A few days later he awoke in his own vomit, naked on his grandfather's roof, staring down at Gramps, who was talking animatedly. It was hard work, but he was going to undo all that she'd learned from Priest and teach her the right way. There was a lot of damage. He told her how to lie on coals in winter, how to find water in the desert, how to live on the outskirts of an unfriendly town. He already had a grunt in his voice, rehearsing to be an Indian. Priest's clothes had holes in them, from where Molly had practiced her shooting by targeting the weathervane. He knew she wanted him dead and didn't blame her.

It took only those six weeks for the old Molly to become submerged within the new kid. Maybe it had started the moment just after she'd yelled "Daddy!" on that day. Maybe there had never been another Molly at all. Priest tried to notice what was happening to her and to care, but he knew he couldn't have made any difference. He couldn't change her mind once it was set on whatever it was set, and he wasn't certain if he should. He realized she was going to get something done, and that he never would.

They sold the house to Septemus for about a quarter of what it was worth. Gramps gave Molly most of the money and sewed it into her vest and jacket and britches, and special pockets in the boots.

By then she didn't look like a boy anymore, but a raging short man that nobody would want to cross, some kind of an afflicted dwarf. She could smile and laugh and you still couldn't see a girl anymore, not even if you were looking, not even if you knew one was supposed to be there. She'd never have any problems playing her role, because it wasn't a role. She could drink whiskey in any bar and get a room in a hotel if she had the cash. Her eyes were chips of shale, and Priest realized that even though he wasn't afraid of his twelve-year-old sister, he should've been.

Gramps gave her a knife, which she kept concealed in the inside pocket of her denim jacket. She carried the Colt and the Remington tucked into her pants, one in front and one at the small of her back, working on her draw. The weight of the weapons meant nothing to her, and neither did the discomfort of carrying them or the possibility they might go off whenever she drew. She'd asked Priest to file off the gun sights so they wouldn't snag, and although he didn't remember doing it he must've, because they were gone.

Molly had ceased to exist in the eyes of Patience. Her friends no longer sought her out, and the schoolmarm did not come around. No one asked about her anymore. It was as natural a thing as watching your parents get murdered in front of you.

"I'm going to Kansas City," she told him.

"What?"

"He's been seen there."

"How do you know?"

"I know."

"How do you know?"

"I've been listening. Lot of marshals and posses have been through the past month. Bounty on him is twenty-five hundred dollars. I'm going to get it."

"You can't. Whatever you're thinking, you can't. I let you go on with it this far because—"

"You didn't have a choice," she said. "None of us does. Besides, I heard Mama last night."

"Molly, that's—"

"She was telling me not to do what I'm going to do on account of her."

Priest's fingers, which hadn't trembled since that day, suddenly began nervously jerking out of place, curling and twisting like they had no bones in them. He'd already had two bottles that afternoon but couldn't fade away, try as he might. Gramps grunted some and stared off in the direction of White Mountain, just waiting to let himself go running in a breechcloth and get shot in the ass.

"But I'm not doing it just for her. It's for me. And for you, in a way, I reckon. Because of the way we are. The way we've got to be." She tried to take hold of his twitching fingers, but they spasmed so badly that he knocked her fist open. "Put Rafe's knife away for now."

He wanted to tell her he wasn't holding the pearl-handled knife, except he was.

"If I don't find him in Kansas City, I'll go where I have to. I'll be back from time to time, to see how you and Gramps are making out."

A quiet but high-pitched titter rose from the back of Priest's throat, as he thought about his sister going after a killer who was already up to twenty-five hundred dollars. Marshals and posses all over the countryside, soon with her in tow, a gun in front and one in back, and she was going to take Yuma Dean down. He glanced all over in a panic, looking for a bottle of whiskey in the usual places but not seeing any under the bed or on the shelf, and no pints in his pockets. Sweat poured off him and he gulped for air, and in his circling brain he stumbled backward, further and further into a burning eddy of darkness but couldn't get free. Her inhuman shale eyes kept after him until his chest felt like it was about to cave in beneath the weight, and as the scream began to work itself loose, she turned and said, "It's all right. It's who you are. Goodbye."

Since then she had taken on a mythical and dreamlike quality, never far from his thoughts but not quite real, not even when he met her on the edge of town, drunk and waiting for her to shoot him in the head.

When Molly stepped out of the coach, he realized just how caught up in the liquor he'd been the other times he'd seen her over the past half a decade. Even with her gunbelt and sunburned cheeks, carrying years' worth of scars and welts, he'd really only recalled her as the glaring twelve-year-old holding the cider cup, when the front door had opened and prickly pear blossoms had come flowing in.

He'd been a damn drunken fool and he hadn't seen her at all.

Molly stood in the door of the coach and waited for the two drivers to set the step and help her down into the street. They each held up a hand and steadied her as she descended, a little shaky on her feet after the long ride, with her belly hampering her some. He wondered if she still carried the guns on her, sitting real low.

They hefted her trunks onto the platform, and Priest said, "Load them into the buckboard. Be careful or you're likely to set off a hell storm of flying bullets."

"Yessir."

The child's voice came up behind him, so distinct in his ear that he nearly spun to take a look. It told him not to turn around, so he didn't, and then whispered, *This is Molly here. This is your sister.*

She had full pink lips set in a worn, sun-browned face, with most of the color beaten from her hair. It was no longer gold, not even yellow really, but only a lifeless shade that had no name. He saw that the tips of her pinkies and top knuckle of the ring finger on her left hand were gone from frostbite. He couldn't see her ears beneath the hat and hair, but he guessed they were probably scarred as well, the lobes missing and cartilage cracked from too many winters lying on nothing but rock.

Molly no longer appeared to be a short angry man—she'd grown into womanhood and didn't need to hide behind anything, not even a bad haircut. Their mother's beauty resided in the angles and softness of her face. Her natural curls draped far past her shoulders, in some places white and in others almost transparent. She tipped her hat back so he could see her face, and he held himself steady beneath her gaze, chin jutting.

Her eyes were blue, slightly too cold, but at least alive. She looked so much like their mother that his breath came out in bites, part of him wanting to go over and lift her and say, "Ma!" He waited for the voice of the child to tell him something more, give him some advice on what to say or do, hoping he could glance around now, but he didn't move.

The moment continued stretching while they stared at each other and the stagecoach driver hovered at Priest's elbow, awaiting compensation. Priest gave him a couple of coins, but the man still didn't leave. Priest handed him a few more, and that just got a huff of air out of the rider. It was all the money Priest had.

A swelling of intense fury washed over him, the pulsing veins darkening at his temples, and he hoped the man could sense the danger. Molly did. She reached into her billfold and took out some cash, and that got rid of the drivers.

"I was the only passenger, and they looked after me real good the whole trip," Molly said. She approached without expression, perhaps feeling just as much as him but controlling it, putting it to use. "Don't get annoyed—they deserved a little extra for feeding me and making extra stops."

With all they had between them, with everything he should be saying, already he'd shown weakness. It took maybe half a minute. A dog would have taken his throat out by now. A surge of shame rippled over him, replacing the anger and leaving him a little sick to the stomach, but it got his feet moving.

He stepped up to her and didn't know what to do with his hands, so he put them on her shoulders. He could feel the tight, hard coils of ropy muscle beneath her oversized shirt. Still, she was petite, and he'd even go so far as to call her dainty. You didn't expect it of someone who'd finished a killer named Sarsaparilla Sam in an ugly fashion for eleven hundred dollars.

Whatever he thought to say sounded stupid, puerile, or silly to him.

"Hello, Molly."

"Hello, Priest."

Seeing her like that was almost like being given a second chance at redemption or forgiveness, and losing it again. He wanted to press his palm over her bulging belly. She was at least eight months pregnant.

Her nostrils flared as she smelled him for liquor. He hadn't had a taste since yesterday afternoon when he'd drunk the laced coffee at Miss Patty's. Molly pursed her lips, a sign that she hadn't taken his being sober for granted. "You look well."

"And you're a beautiful young woman."

She didn't like to hear such things, and her brow furrowed. "Is Grandpa still alive?"

"Yes."

"I'm glad. His ass okay after taking two bullets in it? You told me about it when I was here last."

He couldn't remember anything about the last time he'd seen her except the cool touch of gunmetal and waking up with five hundred dollars jammed into his shirt pocket. "He's all right, and still going Apache, but not at the moment. He has his head about him. It'll do him even more good to see you again."

"You think he'll be right in his mind long enough for me to talk with him?"

Priest didn't know how to explain the fact that Gramps was as right in his mind—or even more so—when he was an Indian, so he let it pass. Maybe she'd be able to have a conversation with the old man that didn't involve *Ga'ns* spirits. "He saw the telegram. It seems to have helped. He's more articulate than usual. I think it's because he knew you were coming."

"I hope that's true. I'd like to have a long talk with him, if I can."

She had an ephemeral accent that wasn't a true accent because it was fleeting and always changing. Sometimes she hung her words like wash out on a line, and sometimes she gave them a musical lilt, a twang, or a ripped cadence. Because she hadn't had much schooling there was a fringe of ignorance, a firm snort of the land not unlike Gramps talking old man's Apache. Priest could hear the Northeast and the South in her, and something like the harsh wind on the open plains, the hardscrabble thirst of the Nations, maybe the autumn passes of the Rockies. What had she lived through?

The sky still churned with black and silver veins, muddled and coiling. More rain in these past two days than in the last six months. Distant thunder grumbling like a beast struggling awake. He slapped the reins, hoping to get home before the storm opened up again, but the buckboard hadn't rolled twenty feet before he had to rear the horse to a stop.

Store signs creaked in the growing wind as Priest sighed, certain that this was going to be a notable scene.

Lamarr stood in the middle of the street, looking only a little worn out after a night with Franny, with his red sash askew and the sombrero a tad crunched and hanging low off the back of his head.

Priest heard a pistol cocking and glanced down to see Molly holding a Walker Colt at her side, shielded by her knee. He didn't know how she could have pulled it so fast, and he hoped his sister didn't shoot Lamarr dead on the spot.

Molly said, "The hell is that?"

"An admirer of yours."

"That right? You mean I've got one?"

"It's the truth."

"Friend of yours?"

"Yep, though he's probably worth a couple hundred back in the East, if you decide you want to bring in a few extra dollars."

"Maybe I'll talk to him first before I make up my mind." She waited for Lamarr to step up, coming around the horse now on her side and taking off his hat, a dew of drizzle building on his shining black cheeks and forehead. Molly held a hand before her eyes and said, "Lord, you're blinding me, man, why'n you frown some for a while?"

" 'Fraid I can't do that none, ma'am," Lamarr said, working his hands around the rim of the sombrero. "I got to follow my heart and state of mind. I just wanted to introduce myself. Lamarr Russell, at your occasional service."

"Only occasionally?"

"Sometimes I'm indisposed or otherwise occupied, but I'd still appreciate it if you allowed me to buy you dinner or a drink after you get yourself settled back in some."

Even Priest raised his eyebrows at that. Molly slowly let the hammer fall back so Lamarr wouldn't notice she held a gun. "Couple years ago, they would've strung us both up in front of the courthouse for something like that. Times change that much since Appomattox?"

"I reckon not. Why, just yesterday morning three peckerwood sumbitches with a rope come calling on me and tried to do ungodly things to a harmless spruce."

"Let me guess," Molly said. "Their mamas are gonna miss all three of 'em at Christmas dinner this year."

Easing his lips back, those glowing teeth showing inch after inch and still not stopping yet, rain running into his mouth and not bothering him a bit. "That surely be the case."

"You're worth two hundred dollars in Virginia City, you know."

"Good God amighty, I never even been in Virginia."

"Maybe it was Memphis."

"Well, I did have a run-in once there with a couple graycoats who done forgot they lost the war. Still startles me down to the tips of my big toes how many folks don't know about Honest Abe's Emancipation Proclermation. No wonder he needed to tip a whiskey now and again. You gonna use that Walker Colt you ain't concealing all that well and turn me in?"

Actually, she'd concealed it perfectly, but Lamarr could surprise you that way, spotting what nobody else could see. Molly grinned, maybe a touch impressed, and said, "That depends. You owe my brother money?"

Priest said, "This I gotta hear."

Lamarr set himself, took a deep breath, and put the sombrero back on. "Not exactly, no, see, it's Fatima who's got the money, and as soon as she let loose on that garter belt some, I swear I'm—"

Priest said, "He owes me money *and* a sombrero."

"That right?"

"Well, I was considering allowin' him to borrow this one right here for when he takes Sarah O'Brien to the spring dance, if'n he washes his hair first."

"I reckon that's taking a step in the right direction. I'll consider engaging some of your service, if you ain't indisposed or otherwise occupied."

"It'd be my honor, Miss McClaren."

"G'day to you, Mr. Russell."

Priest watched Lamarr walk across the street, heading toward downtown where he could get breakfast. Lamarr had a swagger going, and damned if Priest didn't sit forward in his seat staring, checking to see if that really was a skip in his step. It couldn't be, and Priest couldn't watch anymore. He didn't really know what the hell had just happened and was pretty sure he was a lot better off that way.

"Nice fella," Molly said.

They rode in silence, the wheels clattering beneath them and the traffic building all around. Carriages and wagons and lone riders setting out in every direction, the noise filling in until it became so solid that Priest had to shrug his shoulders like he was throwing off a blanket. His hands tingled and he wanted to touch Molly's belly and ask about the father, but he feared she might've been raped, and hearing that right now would pitch him into the dirt.

"You still courting that Irish girl?" she asked.

"On occasion."

She let out a cluck the way Pa might have.

"How do you court someone only on occasion? I can see you and that Lamarr Russell are cut from the same cloth, only doing things *on occasion*. Ain't there anything you do all the time 'cept breathe? If you're gonna court, then you oughta court all the time—else what you doing it for?"

"Sarah said damn near those exact words to me two days ago."

"Smart lady, then."

"Yes," Priest told her, "you both are."

"About some things, I s'pect. If'n you love somebody, you got to put everything else aside."

And spend a good deal of time at the milliner's buying hats. "That isn't always easy."

"Might as well say it's almost impossible. Why there's so many beaten women and castrated men."

"There a lot?"

"More'n I care to mention." The young girl in her bled through for a second, and he almost wished it hadn't. There she was again, hiding just out of sight. "You hear about them mail-order brides they got now? Lonely homesteader wants a wife to darn his socks, cook his meals, help fend off Indians, and bed him while he clears land and builds a lopsided house in the territories. Just writes a letter and asks for a lady's hand, and off she bustles with her ass in a hoop skirt." Molly had taken down a crazed buffalo skinner who'd had two mail-order wives and skinned them both, and Priest could see the fervor with which she went after her quarry. "The hell's idea is that? A third of them get bushwhacked on the way out to the men, and another third cross a thousand miles, stay a couple weeks until the first bear comes around, and then they gotta pack up all their shit and go home again anyways."

"Maybe I should try it," Priest said.

"The mail-order girl that shows up on your doorstep won't even wait for a bear to chase her off."

"What a disagreeable thing to say!"

"Ha!"

And yet Gramps had been so in love, he still curled up with his wife's ghost under the horse trough. Mother could dance to Pa's fiddle even though she was deaf, hearing his passion for the music, the vibrations of his pulsing blood beating in her own heart. Christ, he had to find Sarah.

He figured he'd ask. "You in love?"

"No."

"Ever been?"

"No, but if you think that proves I don't know what I'm talkin' about, you better try harder to shimmy free a the truth."

He'd shimmied out of a lot of things, but hardly ever the truth.

Priest put his arm around his sister and gave her an inept hug, restrained and made even more awkward by his knife and her guns and the fact that neither of them was particularly good at showing emotion. He wanted to cry and did not want to cry. He wished he could hand her a doll and take them both back to the dead past where he had another chance to reach into Pa's drawer. He could feel the burning rage inside her like an overheated furnace about to rupture. There was no childhood left to recover.

Grasping her was like holding on to five years of resistance and rancor, and he could only imagine falling across her lap and weeping up the mistakes of his life while she stroked his hair, Papa's fiddle playing to keep down the fever. Or that Molly would burst into a frenzied sobbing and look up at him with warm eyes again. They both drew back in the same instant, amazed they'd been able to hug at all.

It began to rain harder, and he pushed the horse to go faster. Molly pointed to places and people she recognized, her scarred pinkie sticking out too far. Fifteen men over the last three years, but she hadn't yet found the one who mattered. Did she scream out Dean's name in her nightmares or did she sleep soundly, a part of

185

her soul kept separate despite everything? He wanted to ask but didn't know how to put it into words.

"How do you do it?" he asked.

"I only do what I have to do. No more choice in it than in how tall I am or the color of my eyes. The same holds true for you. Don't scorn yourself for it."

"And you? Do you hate me?"

"No. You hate me?"

"Of course not."

"Well, then," she said, and that was the end of it. "We heading to Gramps's place?"

"Yep. Right up ahead."

"Good, I could do without another spell of pneumonia."

He still lived in Gramps's shack just on the north side of Main Street, close to the colored quarter. Patience would eventually push south with its expansion and swallow this whole seedy section, but it hadn't happened yet. Molly glanced up at the rusted weathervane on the courtesy roof. Priest knew she was thinking about when she'd shot up his clothes.

The wave of shame had not receded and probably never would. He led her inside and went back for her trunks. Lifting one was like lifting the ghosts of fifteen evil men and their bounties. Only seventy pounds of pistols and he nearly tumbled over. He stacked them beside the bed, then rolled and lit a cigarette, waiting for his sister to stop pawing through her memories of this place. They were all bad.

But maybe she felt different about that than he thought. She'd learned what had to be learned here, coming into herself and becoming who she was supposed to be. He'd give up a pinkie and his earlobes for that, if only he could discover what he needed to become.

Gramps wasn't here, which surprised Priest. Gramps had been looking forward to seeing Molly again. He'd even swept the place up and washed the dirty dishes and made the beds.

She said, "This all you own?"

"Yes."

"Everything?"

"Yes."

"You could carry it all in one cheap suitcase. I got more in my trunk." She set her teeth, wanting to ask what he'd done with their parents' possessions. He hadn't taken anything, and sold it all off and gave the money to Padre Villejo's mission. He waited to see if she'd mention their parents first, because he sure as hell wasn't going to.

She said, "Pack it. We're moving."

He didn't argue the point. If she wanted to go elsewhere, he knew she had the money to move into the largest house in Patience, or rent out any number of rooms at the hotel.

"I saw a house for sale in town, about six or eight blocks down from the depot, on Broad Street," she said. "Know where I'm talking about?"

"I think so."

"That place any good?"

"No."

"Why not?"

"The back window faces east. It's right across from Freerson's Dry Goods Emporium. Gramps won't be able to slip out when he goes Apache."

"Why does he do it?"

"Apaches never go insane from fear and pain and heartbreak. They survive anything, and always have."

"Just like us. He didn't have to be an Indian. All he needed to do was stay a damned Mc-Claren."

"He has."

The miles had worn her out. She fought to stay awake, even though her eyes were half lidded.

"Do you want me to get you something to eat?"

The deep smooth musk of her coasted into his nostrils as she attempted to decipher him, one enigma to another. "No."

"You're tired, Molly, and you need to rest.

There are clean sheets on the bed. We'll talk about moving later, if you still want to bother."

"I reckon it don't matter none, huh?"

"I doubt it."

She took off her jacket and carefully placed the guns within easy reach, then lay on the bed on her side with her eyes shut. She held her stomach with a puzzled grimace, as though she had just found it lying there on top of her and didn't know how it had gotten there.

Priest helped to get her boots off. A serenity descended over her, each muscle relaxing one by one in turn, right down from her neck to her calves. It was a trick the medicine men used to help invite their visions.

When she opened her eyes again she had a noncommittal gaze, calm but exact; like her voice. "I couldn't find him, Priest."

"Molly—"

"I tried Fort Thomas and Vera Cruz and Sweetwater. Cedar Rapids and Mud Creek. I been to Denver and Caloosa and Pennsylvania and just about all points in between. I crossed the plains and the Nations—most of them, anyway. Even wound up in the Dakotas during winter, colder than you can imagine. Trust me. Believe me."

"I do. Molly, you're home now."

He sucked air as he said it, realizing it was

about the worst thing he could say, but somehow it had come naturally. He heard a sound, repetitive and familiar, but he couldn't place it. She stared over with a sad smile and talked slowly to him, like he was too thick to understand what she was saying. "This ain't home to me. This is just the place where it started."

He'd never argue with that, but he kept hoping to soothe her—except she was already at ease. "It's okay. We'll make it right."

"You can't."

"We'll try."

"Sometimes I was close," she said. "Think that counts, Priest? To be close? At least sometimes? I was in his tracks. I could smell his sweat."

"Get some sleep, Molly," he told her, doing his best to remember that she was all of seventeen years old. The incessant noise continued and came into better focus. He looked down and saw that he'd been sharpening the knife on a whetstone. "Now it's my turn."

Chapter Twelve

They didn't have to look hard to find six new saloons, all of them put up in the last three months. Most wouldn't serve coloreds, and the two that did had busy faro tables. That would just lead to more calamity. By the time they hit Market Street they were both too tired to care what kind of bar they got near, no matter the consequences. A saloon called the Golden Reception looked nice enough and stood well-lit in the middle of the block. They got a table and a bottle, mindful of only a few sidelong glances and mutters, which was just fine.

Words circled Priest but didn't touch him. Lamarr sat quietly drinking, oddly silent, waiting for Priest to bring it on. Somebody was winning big at poker across the room, where one man's hoots were met with brutal scowls. Both Priest and Lamarr shifted slightly in their seats so they could keep an eye on the action. You never knew when someone might shout cheat and where it would go from there.

Lamarr wanted to play faro, to ride the tiger some more. One hand raised the whiskey glass and the other tapped the table like he was taking cards. Priest didn't mind the money that had been lost, because he hadn't earned it anyway. His sister had brought him bleeding cash. All that puzzled him now was that he'd ever bothered with the store and the shelves and the sign, acting out some part he never could've fit into. What the hell had he been thinking? He couldn't get over it.

The poker player started to lose, and it got the other fellows at the table talking and laughing again. Lamarr scanned the saloon, his head swiveling slowly until his gaze met Priest's. They sort of looked through each other for a moment, abandoned to the drag of their thoughts, drifting.

"I've got to go after him," Priest said.

"She's been at it for five years and she's damned good at what she does. You ain't gonna do no better."

A part of him wanted to hear exactly that, a sensible reason to stay in Patience and continue his quick crawl into oblivion. "I have to try."

"Maybe you do."

"Stopped off at the sheriff's office and squeezed what information I could out of Burke."

"Bet it wasn't too difficult, Burke being the kinda man who likes to let others do his job for him. Anything worthwhile?"

"Not really. Rumor that Dean was in New Mexico. Somebody else said California."

"She didn't come home just to watch you leave."

"I believe she did," Priest said, understanding the reality of the situation, solid as bone. "She can't do it anymore, so far along with child, and someone has to be out there. If she had another choice, any other choice, she'd have gone with it, but she doesn't. In the morning she'll probably hand me the Remington .44 I didn't pull out of the drawer that afternoon."

He'd never mentioned that day to Lamarr before while sober, but knew he'd repeated the facts plenty when he was drunk, babbling in the hog pens. Lamarr said, "Passing it on?"

"Sure. You know as well as I do the importance of something like that. The significance. Or else why sing your mama's slave songs when you're a free man now?"

"We all got us a history."

Not only one, but many. Starting and stopping, veering, with others running side by side down the distance like railroad tracks. Histories entwined, coupled one to another, trailing behind and chasing you from this next step right into forever.

"Strong as your convictions might currently be," Lamarr said, "you're still a prize fool for even thinking any of this."

"That right?"

"I'm gonna be as sensitive to your feelings as I possibly can, but the truth of the matter is that you ain't never slept on no mountainside."

"No."

"Never rode the Devil's Highway with forty miles to go and only a thimbleful of water. You ain't ever even been more'n, what, fifteen or twenty miles outside of this very town."

"That's a fact."

"So how do you aim to travel all the way to California knowin' what you know, which is nothin'?"

"Well . . ."

"You can't do it."

As if there was any other choice now, like he could back out and head left or right or sideways. Rebuild the store and put up another sign, stand there in the street again with piles of pine sawdust swirling around his ankles. Priest started getting hot, pouring himself doubles and sucking the liquor slowly against his teeth. "True, I never strangled a plantation master or fought in a war . . ."

"Be damn thankful of that, son," Lamarr said mildly, with a grim diamond glint.

". . . but I still need to do this."

"What about Sarah? Chances are you gonna miss that spring dance you been waitin' on."

And there was a question, wasn't it? One that went through the meat and straight on to the marrow. What about Sarah? What about the child? Except there was no child. "I'll tell her goodbye tonight."

"You will, eh?"

A jab thrown there, Lamarr telling him he couldn't do it. Lamarr didn't know that it was already pretty much done, and had been for a while. "Yes."

"It's almost ten o'clock. That's when she steps on stage, right?"

"Listen, you'd better stay away from your proud pappy for the time being, seeing as how he tried to skewer you."

"He was just funnin' is all."

They poured another and downed them quickly, each pulling something extra from the bottle: a last bit of flavor or a soothing flush of heat. Priest wouldn't leave Lamarr alone to face

Septemus and Griff after the last fracas, so whatever needed to be done would have to be done tonight. That was all right—everything could be cleaned up at once, and then he could leave town and find and kill Yuma Dean, the way he should've years ago.

Lamarr slowly got to his feet, one hand out as if to push Priest back into his chair or to help him up. "It surely has been a while since I seen any of California, and Fatima's sister, Rosina, works at a fine dance hall there called the Kitty Kat Palace up in San Francisco. Been meaning to stop in and look her up again, and from experience I can honestly say her garter ain't quite so tight as her sister's."

"Watch over Molly for me."

Lamarr acted like he didn't hear and would continue to do so, no matter what Priest said. He could just as easily have told him that Molly didn't need any looking after, and had never had anybody to look after her before anyway, so why start now.

They rode across town to the Home Hearth Theater. Moonlight caught in Lamarr's white hair, making the patches shine but not his teeth. He would sporadically let out a gruff laugh, but he wasn't smiling. Priest thought he could smell blood. He knew he might have to kill Griff tonight. He would do it—if he could—because he finally had gotten what he'd yearned for but had been too afraid to go after. A larger fate, Chicorah had called it, maybe a life he could put to some use even if he didn't know how to survive the Devil's Highway or make a proper bedroll. If he was lucky, Gramps would give him a few pointers before he left.

As always, Septemus Hart sat in his seat of honor in the balcony, not sipping sherry tonight but drinking from a chalice, a goddamn silver *chalice*. The purple shirt was finely ruffled beneath his gray Confederate coat, and the saber still swung at his side. He looked drunk and wildly happy, and even Griff had a flicker of joy in his frigid stare. That worried Priest.

"Damn," Lamarr said, "looks like the party's still going on."

"Something else."

Priest looked around at the scouts, easterners, and cowpokes, and saw several more Mex faces tonight, the newly hired vaqueros who'd brought in the stolen herd of the murdered Don Carlos Herrera Villejo, everybody kicking it up pretty good. Septemus's other guests, the Federales and army generals, were raising hell on their two-day drunk. Miss Patty's house would be packed tonight, and Wainwright would have his hands full disarming these jaspers one after another.

Sarah already stood on stage, surrounded by

the proscenium and those thick burgundy curtains, commanding attention with her Irish gaze. She wasn't wearing a hat, and that startled him. A shard of ice slid between his ribs and twisted.

The stomp of her heels keeping time against the shining wood sounded louder than he expected. She no longer appeared childlike or lost before the crowd, but instead seemed on the verge of something else as she began to sing, full of confidence and quality.

Despite the usual bedlam of the room, the audience quelled to an immediate silence. Priest shifted his stance, and you could hear the floor creak under him. The song wasn't one of the banal ones Septemus normally chose for her, it was "When My Love Fills My Arms Under Heaven," Priest's favorite. The brogue came on stronger than usual, the way it did after she talked to her father for a few hours. Her words gathered power as they spanned the distance between them, hurtling forward like a fist and taking him high in the heart.

"Lord, that's a lovely sound," Lamarr said, leaning as he listened. "She done come into her own."

He was right. There was a difference to her voice, a fullness that hadn't been there before. There was something wrong about her, an attribute that didn't quite fit, or at least hadn't fit before. He kept letting his gaze rove over her, up and down, catching on whatever wasn't right but still unable to figure it out.

Priest glanced up at the balcony and Lamarr looked back over his shoulder. Septemus smiled down on them and waved.

Lamarr's jaw hung so low it actually cracked. "Jesus, God of my soul, take me in your sweet hands and bring me to the throne, 'cause I done seen it all now."

"You and me both."

"Let's go find out what the hell this is about."

They took the stairs three at a time. Priest kept his hands balled into fists to make sure he didn't go for the blade without thinking. Lamarr let out the gruff laugh again like a blow to the stomach when they stepped up to the private purple area that smelled of roast pig. The Federales were stuffing themselves and swaying to the music. Septemus sat with the chalice to his mouth, taking long loud sips of wine. Priest felt a heavy draw of anguish and still didn't know why, though he realized he'd find out soon enough.

"I suppose you're here to offer your congratulations," Septemus said, presenting silver goblets.

Lamarr had another tall drink with his short daddy. It was becoming a regular habit. "I'll say yes, because I know you're a man constantly worth congratulating."

"That may be the most honest comment you've ever passed."

"Or might be the biggest lie."

"In any case, let's have more wine!"

Septemus broke into giggles while they drank. Priest tried hard to concentrate on Sarah's song, hoping to pinpoint what was wrong or only different. The ebb and flow of distress continued to churn inside him. Griff kept a wide smile, too, and used a thumb to scratch his chin, the other arm across his chest with the hand wedged into his armpit. Priest had never seen a gunny so sure of himself, always keeping his fingers so far from his triggers.

"Let me guess," Priest said. "It has to do with fresh beef."

"Not at all!"

"Land acquisition?"

"No!"

But of course it didn't. A man like Septemus Hart didn't smile over money. He might kill for it, but he'd never smile over it.

"But you've come into some more good fortune?" Lamarr asked.

"Yes!"

"Well, ain't that nice."

"I'd say so!"

Lamarr let his beaming teeth show, row after row rolling out mile after mile. "Leave a dead old man behind, Daddy?"

Another happy titter. "Now now, you nigger bastard, there'll be none a that."

After finishing his wine, Lamarr sighed and turned to Priest. "I done think I've lost all his respect."

"It's a distinct possibility."

Lamarr cupped his ear. "You hear that? Listen close. I do believe that's the sorrowful sound of my heart shattering to pieces."

Priest cupped his ear too. "Will you think any less of me if I fall to my knees weeping now?"

"In fact, I might join you."

Griff locked his eyes on Priest's. That genuine glow of elation from Septemus had enveloped the gunny, making him show his dimples. Christ, he had dimples. Griff took a step forward and whispered, "Met a fella like you once in Omaha. Orphan, always talking about his daddy, couldn't settle on any woman but was carrying on crying blue lonesome just waiting for somebody to come along to put a bullet in his head. I got a pal I haven't seen in five years coming into town tomorrow who done helped that old boy in Omaha. Helped him out real good. Guess my friend would enjoy himself a good deal abetting you too."

201

"You've got a friend?"

Priest frowned, thinking about it. If Griff was going to take the time to insult him, then he wasn't about to go through with killing him right now. That wouldn't be his play. The joy in his eyes meant something, and he wanted to burn Priest with it for as long as he could. With an immense effort, keeping his hand from the knife handle, Priest decided to wait it out.

He almost stabbed Griff to death anyway. Sarah's song was coming to an end, and he tried to listen to the timbre of those lyrics, to find the meaning within them. When he saw the move, he pulled the blade halfway out and had to force himself to slide it back into the sheath.

In a blur of black motion Griff drew his pistol and pressed it into Priest's belly. He reholstered it and pulled his gun loose again with amazing speed, jamming the barrel into Priest's chest. Even faster now, he replaced the gun and invisibly whisked it high to jab Priest in the forehead, drawing the hammer back nice and slow.

This was salve to Griff's ego. He'd been latched to Septemus's side for so long that he didn't want to backslide into the real life of the gunny he'd once been. A few show-off tricks were good enough to heal his pride damaged from that kick to the chin. They were getting there, but some blood had to run. Priest waited, giving a slight shake of his head to Lamarr so he wouldn't do anything stupid now that the venom was splashing all over.

With his saber clinking, Septemus stood and toasted them. Griff holstered his pistol and drew it one last time, bringing it back and slapping it against the side of Priest's head. Priest's brain flushed with liquid shapes as Septemus guffawed and slapped his thigh, reaching out to pat Griff on the shoulder with one hand and Priest on the back with the other.

Blood dripped down the side of Priest's face, but he managed to grin. There are times you just have to ride it out and see what happens next. It was fine now.

Septemus threw Priest a linen cloth to clean himself with. "That's enough. No more fighting for the time being. This is a celebration."

"You still rejoicing your birthday?" Lamarr made a good show of yawning, loosening his neck and shoulders. "Funeral yesterday for Don Carlos sort of drained my spirits. Seems a bunch of back-shooting, night-riding cattle rustlers done butchered him."

"We live in mean times." Septemus smiled, letting it out slow, tooth after tooth, exactly like Lamarr did. Seeing them like that, turning their faces toward one another with that same perfect smirk, scared the hell out of Priest.

"Not so bad for some." Lamarr found some grapes on a plate and started popping them into his mouth. "Not just anyone who can throw a three-day-long birthday party now."

Sarah finished singing, and the applause erupted. Septemus placed his small thick hands together clapping, no longer giving his standard half-minute. He let it loose, stomping his heels, the bastard actually whistling. Griff did the same, waving his hat but keeping an eye on Priest, leering at him and waiting for something to hit. Okay, so here it is.

"This is a different celebration," Septemus said, and chuckled, allowing the sound to fill his throat all the way to the top before it came bubbling out, wet and ugly.

"Yeah?"

"Yeah! It's my wedding!"

Priest whirled. Sarah stood watching him in the balcony as the applause continued to roar around her. Now he saw it.

She was wearing a diamond ring.

Chapter Thirteen

The voice of the child told him he should have expected this, the signs had been there forever, but he hadn't seen it coming at all. Not even with her mentioning Septemus's proposal, and not when his gaze had roamed over her.

The child continued talking, high and excitedly, but Priest was too numb to hear any more. He wandered down the balcony stairs stinking of his own blood, the wound at his temple still dripping and spattering the carpet. Sarah sang several more songs while he waited in the back row, her shadow huge and looming against the curtains, an immense dark hand on the ceiling, descending.

He saw the ring clearly now as the footlights

refracted through the diamond, sending a rainbow scattered against the orchestra pit. Red fell on the drummer's frenetic face, a deathly green washing over the trumpeter's skin like scales. A lissome violet smeared across the first two rows of drunks, their teeth purple and shining. The anguish made greater sense now, condensed under his heart but struggling around some, like a roused animal.

Vaqueros recognized him as he moved through the crowd, but no one approached. The McClaren madness clung to him in all its distinction, and for the first time he appreciated the fact that he was beyond himself and nothing could touch him here. He tried to get a drink, but no one would meet his eyes or come near enough to serve him. A quarter-full bottle of whiskey sat on a table, and without fully realizing it he reached over and drank it.

There were three miners staring up at him, but no one said anything. Priest knew he held the knife in his other hand, though he didn't feel it there. Its weight and substance remained only in his memory. He wanted to use it badly. Some ghosts were beyond you and some were right up close, made of honed steel. The wound at his temple had stopped trickling, but the stench of blood worsened. He began to enjoy it.

Septemus's hoots wafted over the Home

Hearth, and the vaqueros and everybody else stomped even louder. There was something obscene and unholy stirring in the night, everyone catching hold of the lunatic mood. If Sarah stepped off the stage right now, she would pay for the blunder with her life. They'd tear her open like a laden water skin and wouldn't stop until there was nothing left of her to rend.

If Padre Villejo, having left the mission for the first time in nine years, had swung among them in this minute, he would've used his crutches to fling aside the bodies of the butchers who had murdered his beloved uncle. If Chicorah had slipped silently inside, weaving among them as quiet as a snake until the time to strike, he would've taken down a dozen of the men who liked scalping renegades. But now only Priest stood here, or only a part of himself, and he had another priority.

The houseman slid away, and Priest stepped backstage into a place he did not belong and never would. A larger fate had its price, and already the cost was too much to bear intact and unaltered. He had lost Sarah a long time ago, or she had lost him. He could stand that, but he didn't think he could bear knowing that Septemus Hart would go to bed with her each night. How he would smooth his hands down the soft angle of her tilted jaw and run his greasy lips over her glossy white and pliant belly.

At her door he paused, trying to fight through the overwhelming dream that this, none of *this*, was happening or had ever happened.

He didn't see the door open, but it had, and he was inside her dressing room, toe to toe with Sarah. His knees had gone watery, and he hoped to Christ that he'd put the knife away. He looked down and saw that he had.

Sarah O'Brien, his lost beloved, stared at him with eyes of black embers, defiant but at ease. Her hair curled and swept wildly about her shoulders, and she inclined her head first one way and then the other, in tune with the movement and tide of those tresses. It had been so long since he'd seen her hair hang freely, without the encumbrance of a hat, that he hadn't realized she'd let it grow so very long.

The diamond threw sparks of tinted illumination all around the room. When she turned and the colors hit him, he backed off as if mule-kicked.

"And so it's now you've come to talk?" she asked.

"I've been looking for you for days."

"Not nearly as long as I once searched for you, Priest McClaren."

So she would be direct while he writhed. Priest

saw how this affected her, the lack of strain in her face. Her hands were loose on his elbows, the way you would touch a stranger you once liked but no longer cared for, although you wanted him to keep thinking you did. Her mouth drew into a warm and languid smile, the tip of her tongue pink and showing. He didn't exactly understand why she wasn't upset, except that, possibly, she was truly happy. He tried to wrap his mind around that possibility, but it was too great for him to grasp. Sarah's midnight eyes still smoldered, and he wanted to back away from them, retreating from the blackness like nothing he'd ever feared before.

"What's the matter, Priest McClaren?" she asked.

"You're asking me that?"

"Well, yes, of course I am, my boyo. Are you surprised at that?"

"Sarah—"

"You haven't been able to say the right thing to me for ages, and even now, with all you're feeling, you still don't feel nearly enough."

"I do."

"What is it you've come to say?"

He didn't have any idea. For a second it seemed as if she might let him embrace her, but she did a quick sidestep and glided away. He followed, and she moved again, as if they were idly dancing.

"Tell me now, Priest McClaren, what is it that's rushing through your mind? That I'm a fool for marrying Septemus Hart? Are you damning me in your very soul? Or only yourself?"

She spoke as if enraged, but there was no temper there. It had been cleansed from her, possibly by him, perhaps by Septemus, but it was gone.

They continued to unravel. She moved toward him, and Priest had to hold a hand out to stop her where she stood. She was petite, but she had a real strength that could still surprise him as she pushed forward until her lips were nearly on his. This wasn't pettiness or loathing. She had found an answer and wanted to pass it on to him, but there was simply no way it could be done.

"And what of us?" he whispered.

What the hell was he saying? He had come here to refuse her, and, finding she'd denied him first, now he begged.

"I asked you once of your intentions, Priest. You said to me that you weren't sure. That alone told me all I needed to know about us, despite our years."

"Are you in love with him?"

He didn't expect any hesitation, and there

wasn't one. "No," she said, "but nothing is worse than loneliness."

"Don't marry him, Sarah. Find someone else if you must, but wait for somebody you love."

"I did wait for a man I loved, and he never came for me."

He rocked onto the balls of his feet as if someone had just broken his jaw. Sweat crept through his hair and his scalp prickled, but his throat went dry. He thought he could learn to go Apache now, and wondered how much longer it would take for him to wind up under a trough crying, *Sarah, Sarah.*

"You deserve more than Septemus Hart."

"And what do you know of it? He owns everything, so how can there be more?"

He could only think to say he was sorry, but his words failed him, as they should have. How to tell her of Molly's return, the advent of his larger fate, the voice of their child, and these memories of his bleeding parents. She knew so much of it already, but not all, and not nearly enough. There was nothing to do.

"You've your own life to lead, Priest," she told him. That hair, that beautiful untamed hair veering and coiling everywhere. "Perhaps I've been holding you back all this long time. You need to find assurance and commitment elsewhere. Wherever it is, surely it hasn't been with me."

"That's not true. Don't make light of what we've shared."

"I would never do any such thing."

But she had, or so he thought. "And you?" he asked. "Are you happy?"

"Don't ask me any more foolish questions. I'm not one to believe in girlish fancies anymore. We're going to be married next week."

"That's not you talking, Sarah, that's Septemus."

She glanced at Priest then and he hoped to see some ire there, that Irish fury animating her toward argument until the blue veins stood out of her neck. He could see it happening as their passion rose, and they could forget the talk and make love inside the moment, letting the rest, whatever that might be, fall away to nothing. Instead she let out a low satisfied laugh, and for the first time in years appeared perfectly contented. She struggled to keep from shaking her head in misery for him.

"You're a grave man, Priest. You always have been. There's more killing in you than in any ten others I've ever known."

"I've never killed anyone," he said.

"You will. For so very long I thought my love could draw you from that dark place, but you weren't willing to leave. You've taught me you must do what you must, and it's a lesson I learned late but learned well."

She sounded so much like Miss Patty that he lost himself for a second, unsure of where he was. But despite the life Patty had led, even she never sounded so recklessly sharp.

Grinning, Sarah turned back to the mirror, primping her hair as if she hadn't seen it in a long time and was as shocked by its length as Priest had been. This was only another step, possibly the last one, on her way to being completely rid of him.

By inclination or perhaps intention, those fingers rose to her curls once more until the diamond hooked the light again, dragging it forward. When the colors dropped on Priest he was already rushing for the door—yet not nearly fast enough, as they engulfed him.

He burned and ripped himself free to run from the theater, as cold and scraped out as any dead man settled in his grave.

Chapter Fourteen

Prickly pear petals followed him inside as he paused in the doorway, metallic moonlight streaming around his boots like rushing water. The night was gusting and the windows rattled violently in their frames, each cracked piece of glass buzzing. The lamp had been lit but turned so low that it took a minute to adjust to the darkness in the room. Priest quietly shut the door.

Gramps stared down at Molly while she slept, stroking her face and whispering or perhaps singing softly to her. He crouched near the headboard in a breechcloth, grunting once in Priest's direction, his long white hair tied back with a headband.

He'd never made the switch so quickly before.

It usually took three or four months of the white life to wear him down into an Indian again.

Together they watched the steady rise and fall of her chest as she softly snored and murmured in her sleep, each of them fascinated with her very nearness. The dynamics of their family had changed with the occupancy of another life among them here in the squalid shack. The blood ties were stronger than ever before, now that she'd returned to them. Priest turned up the lamp so he could look into his grandfather's eyes, and he saw that the old man had been crying. Neither of them wanted to leave her, yet here they were both going.

But first Gramps had a message to give. He started gesturing and speaking in Apache, trying desperately to tell Priest something important. At least something that Gramps felt was important.

Priest heard Chicorah's name several times but couldn't make out any kind of context. Gramps kept pointing toward White Mountain, folding his arms and tilting one hand up and then down, a sign for the sun setting. He was really going at it, acting out a grandiose scene that could've been just about anything from a buffalo hunt gone bad to Cochise's last stand. Priest had about lost all patience for this kind of shit, and for the first time he wanted to grab the coot and shake his split memory back into place.

It was time to take it a step further. He started packing, talking the entire time. There was a quiver in his voice he didn't like, but he couldn't growl it loose. "Okay, Gramps, if we're going to be at cross-purposes here, let me tell you a few things. I'm leaving tonight to hunt and kill Yuma Dean, like I should've five years ago. Molly is going to be staying here for the time being, and soon she'll buy a much bigger and nicer place for the two of you and the baby. You're gonna have to turn white sooner than you planned, because I need you here to look after her."

The panes clicked like the fingers of children tapping. "Go take care of whatever business you've got and then get back here, but remember that I'm not going to be around to dig bullets out of your ass anymore. You and I have got responsibilities we've let slide for too long."

Gramps rocked back and looked as though somebody had just hit him in the face with a belt buckle. He whimpered what might've been "My God," and crawled out the window.

Priest held a hand to Molly's belly and dipped low across the bed and pressed his cheek to her the way he once had to Sarah, back when he'd been a daddy for a whole week. He wanted to feel the baby kick or toss, but it didn't. Still, he could feel it there just beyond the thin barrier of skin and fluid and muscle. He hoped he'd get back before Molly's child turned two or three. It seemed consequential to find himself a place in the kid's life by then or he might never be accepted as family, just some stranger the child would look at with wild, puzzled eyes. He no longer had to stand guard over an empty house, because it would never be empty again.

Gramps had disturbed a few coyotes on the edge of town as he headed for White Mountain, and the animals bellowed a melancholy tune. Priest packed up enough gear to keep him going in the desert for at least a week. Food and water, his bedroll and tent makings. He considered going through Molly's trunk and finding a better gun than his own. She had all makes and models, and one of them would fit his hand better, but the answer didn't lie within any other pistol.

This was the hour to turn and face. He bent and kissed the sister he did not know anymore and said, "Sell all these damn guns, Molly—you don't need them anymore."

He shut the window Gramps had gone through and closed the door behind himself as he left. There were more sounds in the night besides those of the coyotes. That cry from Mother when Rafe plunged the knife into her continued in his ear. Priest didn't feel as if he were going anywhere, and he wondered if that was only the fear trying to mire him in Patience.

Despite the recent rain, the night was hot and dry, with the burning wind blowing in from the west. The storm was still there, swirling above. He was almost out of town, nearing the trail, but the voice of the child came in clearly behind him, telling him he wouldn't make it. Moans and whistles made the roan nervous as the smoke trees shook and waved all around.

A presence distinguished itself in the shadows. Priest could feel some familiar aspect making itself known to him, one instant nothing and the next allowing itself to be acknowledged behind a copse of ironwood shrubs. Priest waited and heard the slow clatter of hoofs against rock, the sound drifting over the outcroppings above the road.

Starlight draped the embankments and dust, exposing the world in a sparse silver glory. A pounding drum began, steady and growing louder as Chicorah appeared from out of the darkness upon his horse in all rightful nobility. It gave Priest some small measure of what the world had once been like before Apacheria had crumbled into the rez. The drum was the slamming of his own heart.

Chicorah brought his white-splashed bay pony beside Priest's roan and sat there silently, staring at the moon. It went on like that for a while, maybe an hour or two, while the heated wind stiffened and blasted.

Finally Chicorah asked, "Are you trying to leave?"

"I am leaving."

Nodding now, thinking about that, another lengthy pause between them. "I have something to say about that."

"All right. But let me ask you first: What're you doing out here?"

"Listening to the voices of my gods in this bluster."

"They saying anything worthwhile?"

A strange smile played against Chicorah's lips, the kind of grin just about everybody had been giving Priest lately. Truth be known, he was getting a little sick of it. "If I told you, you would not believe me."

"Yes, I would."

The carved angles and planes of his face sharpened even further as he clenched his jaws. "Yes, that is true. You would."

"Are your gods always right?"

"I do not know. I never heard them before tonight."

He could tell Chicorah about the voice of the child, and how it did not lie and was always much smarter than he was himself, but there didn't seem much point in bringing it up now.

"Why are you alone?" he asked.

"Why are you?"

Apaches didn't toss questions out for lack of having anything better to say, so there was meaning in it. Priest said, "I've relied too much on others my whole sorry life to carry a burden rightfully mine."

"The big black would have rode with you if you had asked."

"And even when I didn't."

"Do you not respect his wishes?"

"Lamarr has other obligations, whether he admits to them or not."

Chicorah seemed to feel that Priest's actions were abnormal because they were more Apache than white, which explained something about the McClaren madness but not much about their reasoning. "You still want blood. And it will come to you."

"I only wish Dean would make it easy for me."

Chicorah let out a laugh, maybe because of what Priest had said or maybe from something his gods were telling him. It didn't much matter.

The bone-handled blade glowed in the moonlight. "Gramps had a hell of a lot to remark about you. You feel like telling me what it was all about?"

"Hart is going to die tomorrow night."

He'd figured it was something like that. "Lamarr might have something to say about it."

"No, he will have nothing to say. He has other *obligations*. He pretends to be different from you, but he is very much like you. He gloats in the face of his enemies and his pain. He enjoys his suffering too much to allow it to end by his own hand."

Priest didn't much like the way it had been put, but in the end he supposed he agreed on the point. "How many braves are you taking?"

"Three." A touch of shame or disappointment tinged the words of the oldest son of the subchief Sondeyka. "There are few warriors left, and most of them I do not trust."

Priest didn't want to see Chicorah die, but there was no possibility that four bucks could match up to the army Septemus had surrounded himself with. Chicorah probably didn't mind that much, seeing the way things were going on the San Carlos rez. It would do him good to bring down his adversary, even if it meant his life. Priest could understand that, but he didn't like it, and with every other thing going on, this was just one more edge taking a layer off his back. He let out a sorrowful sigh, and the night sighed back at him.

"My grandfather will help you. He might be crazy, but he's loyal."

"I know that. And he is not insane. He is blessed."

"I won't argue the point. He has survived in whatever manner he was able."

"That is why he is such a fine Apache. We have not got much power in our medicine anymore, but what we have I will use." He wasn't angry even while on the verge of murder and forfeit and sacrifice. After all his people had suffered this new trespass meant little, but it meant enough to die for.

"How many have been hurt?"

"Three raped women in the last week, one who is a grandmother. They all wandered too far from their jacales because they found deer spoor."

Priest could imagine the vaqueros and ranch hands wounding deer and dragging them up to the mountain as bait, letting the starving women chase them down to feed their dying families.

"The world is getting smaller," Chicorah said after a deep breath. He straightened in his saddle, and his eyes took on a faraway stare as the wind savagely whipped his coiling hair all over. "I was wrong."

"When?"

"I was wrong to burn your store."

"No, you weren't."

"It is not my place to make another find him-

222

self. I presumed too much. For my error in judgment, we suffer."

You live in a world of superstition every minute of your life, but who expects to become myth or hear about from a leader of his people? "You saying your troubles are because of me?"

"Your grandfather is blessed, and whether you choose to believe so or not, so are you."

Priest didn't let the word "blessed" throw him. He knew he'd just been called akin to the devil. "With all you got going on, the pain and hunger and government lies, and you're worrying about me and Gramps? That's sour magic."

"But powerful."

"Your people should never have listened to your gods—they're a mite foolish bunch."

"Or perhaps it is they who are truly insane. It would explain much." He tugged the reins and spun the bay pony away. "We will await you on the north ridge above the hacienda tomorrow night at dusk."

The hell did he say that for?

"I won't be here," he called after Chicorah, but already there was nothing but surging shadows.

Priest sat alone for a while longer, trying to put it all together. The sky started to open up again. Things should've been making sense by now, but there was even more confusion than before he found his larger destiny. He nudged the roan forward.

The horse hadn't even gotten up to a trot before he heard a stagecoach ahead of him, coming into town late. A woman's giggling shriek slashed through the quiet rain, and even the roan looked up. Foolish to keep a lamp lit inside a coach—one rock and the flame could set the whole stage on fire. One of the canvas curtains parted, letting out a thin ray of lamplight that lit the black words painted across three planks nailed together: WELCOME TO PATIENCE. A man laughed.

Priest looked up into the coach's lighted window, seeing a woman's hand turning palm out, revealing one side of her smiling face.

An empty bottle of whiskey flew from the coach and brushed over the roan's left ear. The drapes closed again. Priest reined the horse to a stop and listened to the stage splash through the mud and down into town, until there was only stillness except for the wind. He sighed deeply and didn't move.

In a few minutes he heard crazed laughter ringing all around him. It took a while longer to realize he was the one making all the noise. The horse started to get edgy, standing out in the rain like that, and eventually spun slowly around and headed back to town on its own accord.

The man's voice, that bark of malevolence.
Priest began to tremble.
Christ. Oh Jesus *Christ*.
"My God."
It had been Yuma Dean.

Chapter Fifteen

He didn't know how long he'd been standing in front of Lamarr's shack before Lamarr heard some stray sounds and came outside and got him. Priest wasn't sure what kind of noises he'd been making, whether giggling or crying or talking to himself, only that Lamarr kept saying, "Here, lay yourself down, you're spooking the horses."

Priest lay on the bed with all his clothes on and listened to the spruce rap the window on the other side of the room. He had a hell of a time shutting his eyes, and wound up staring for hours at a ceiling made of notched logs sealed with boards instead of mud. There wasn't a tree for twenty miles around, but somehow Lamarr had found them and felled them and dragged them back here, because it's what he'd learned on the plantation.

Every once in a while Lamarr's face would fill his field of vision and a great black hand would descend against Priest's face and gently try to shut his eyes for him but couldn't. A heavy Georgian drawl like a stream of honey worked in and out of Lamarr's voice. He was being so serious, sounding more and more like his mama. "You jes' hit a rock in the road, ain't no trouble at all wit dat. We in double harness now, me and you, both of us pulling together. Mornin' light gonna show us the way."

Priest liked the sound of the words and wished he could've heard his own mother talk like that, full of melody and grit. Eventually Lamarr fell asleep in his chair and Priest continued to watch the notched wood above him, listening to the clouds bursting, wanting to roll over on his side but unable to get there. The blade seemed to thrum with life, quivering with joy at the approach of its previous master. Blood called to blood. Priest put his fist on the pearl handle and let the trembling, which might have been his own, rock him into sleep.

When he awoke he was already seated with Lamarr at the table, with a half-eaten plate of sausage and eggs in front of him, a cup of coffee in his hand. Priest turned his face aside until his eyes got used to the sunlight streaming in. Lamarr was across from him, finishing biscuits and gravy. They were in the middle of a conversation, and finally the shock of hearing Yuma Dean's laughter was wearing off. Priest ate his breakfast while Lamarr spoke.

"At least you don't need to ride out on the Devil's Highway. I found it questionable you might make it off there alive."

"I know. So did I."

"You didn't even fill your canteen all the way."

The feeling had come back to him slowly, but now he was more relaxed than he could remember ever being before. With the newfound composure came a need to talk, and Priest told Lamarr everything that had happened last night from the moment he'd left Septemus's balcony. Lamarr sat quietly, taking it all in, but getting a little nervous too. He believed in portents and symbols, and there had been too many of them the last two days to overlook.

"A powerful amount of signs."

Calm continued to descend on Priest. Every muscle softened in a flow of warmth from the center of his chest. His thoughts sharpened as more pieces knitted together to form the entire trail his life had taken. No signs were needed anymore. The dead past had finally turned aside long enough to come completely into focus. The child's voice was gone, and he didn't think he'd ever hear it again. It had helped him along about as far as it could.

"My mama once told me I had the mark of Cain upon me, and I was doomed to live a hard life. 'Course, every nigger in a cotton field got the mark of Cain on him. Brand of the whip." Lamarr shook his head, thinking about it all. "You, though . . . hell . . . lawdy . . ."

"He was laughing," Priest said. "He sounded happy. In the coach with that woman."

"Figured he'd be dead or in prison for good by now. Living like a cornered rat if he was alive at all."

"Seems he's had a turn of fortune."

"Time to turn it back some."

"I'd say."

"Still, maybe you should tell Molly."

"She's fitting to burst, and you want her chasing after Yuma Dean."

"She's earned the right. And the way I hear it, she could take him holding a baby in each arm."

It was true. They both deserved to kill Dean, but Priest felt himself competing with his own sister, who'd given up her whole youth to the hunt. She'd done so much in her attempt to avenge their parents, and all he'd managed to do was stumble around drunk for a few years, burn down a shop he never would've opened anyway, and lose his lady and some of his mind. He had so much to make up for.

"It'd be too easy for her," Priest said.

"That's a fair bit of presumption."

"I want to make it count."

If anybody could understand that, Lamarr could. Always smiling bright enough to blind a man, but with the fury roiling just beneath. He could've killed Septemus easily whenever he liked, but first he had to squeeze his short daddy, let him breathe, and then crush him some more.

Lamarr poured whiskey into his coffee but didn't offer any to Priest. He sipped slowly, nodding, letting it come to him. "A man like Yuma Dean, that kind of price on his head, runs out of room to move even on the range, but now why would he come on back here to Patience?" He tussled it around, making the connections where they'd fit. His head lifted. "My, my, my. Could have something to do with Septemus's sociable birthday gathering. And all the Mex officials."

"It does. He's friends with Griff."

They were getting all the way down to it. Lamarr soon let out the slow slide of his smile, and all of it was for blood. "In the balcony—"

"Griff said he had a friend coming back into town he hadn't seen in five years."

All this time and Priest had been missing only the smallest clue. The bank job had been a bust—

Grave Men

they hadn't gotten away with much money. Priest clearly recalled the saddlebag bulging with notes and documents but hardly any cash.

"Griff helped Dean and Spider Rafe rob the bank in Patience five years ago. They split up, and Griff must've run into Septemus at the time."

"Got hisself a better job."

"And now that Septemus might be looking to cut himself a part of the pie south of the border, he needs more men to help him hold the vaqueros and cowhands in line."

"Keeps Griff at his side here, and uses ol' Yuma Dean to oversee his new action in Mexico?"

Priest couldn't get all the way around the notion that Dean had come back willingly. Laughing, drunk, and with a woman. Who the hell knew? Maybe he'd been in town many times before, living out at the rancheria, helping Septemus expand his fortune and solidify his power. And Septemus and Griff had known about it the entire time, offering sanctuary to the murderer of his parents.

"Looks like all accounts gonna be settled tonight," Lamarr said. "What you might call serendipitous. I sorta like the idea of that."

"Me too, actually."

"And the Apaches are attacking the Hart ran-

231

cheria tonight. How many of them?"

"Three. And Gramps."

"And us."

"Yep."

"Against all them boys."

"Yep."

"Wonder if there's any cake left."

Lamarr got out his carbine and his converted .36 Navy revolver, pushed aside the breakfast plates, and started the slow process of breaking apart the weapons and oiling them. Priest went out to his horse, got his pistols out of his saddle-bag, and laid them next to Lamarr's. He'd never been much good at cleaning guns, and Lamarr seemed to be enjoying himself, humming slave songs.

Priest sat back and began sharpening the knife on a whetstone.

They went deep into their work, already pining for the night. The stone threw sparks, and Lamarr's singing must've got him thinking about the plantation again. His fingers flexed like they were tightening around a man's neck. "Gotta say one thing about Septemus. He hasn't thought small since he got run out of Georgia with his pants down."

"You know, you would have saved everybody a lot of trouble if you'd just caught up with him in the field and killed him that day."

Lamarr shook his head, genuinely sorrowful as his lungs worked like a bellows and drove out a long, downhearted breath. "Damned if I don't already know it."

Chapter Sixteen

They were about two miles out of the north ridge of the hacienda, wedged into an outcropping of the sandstone bluff that bordered the rez. This was most likely the area that the wild hands had staked out in order to chase after Apache women. There were scuff marks on the rock, and at least one horse had lost a shoe.

Lamarr was still humming, and Priest had learned enough of the tune to hum along with him. The red wash of the fading sun threw flinching shadows of wind-whipped greasewood along the precipice. It was still a couple of hours before sunset, but the storm kept at it and the gray sky now loomed threaded with darkness, the rains coming down in staggered eruptions in the heat.

The calm was still there, but not as settled as it had been earlier. His thoughts returned again and again to Sarah, with her long hair unfurled around her shoulders, and all that black severity in her eyes. She did not love him and hadn't for a long time, but if Septemus died tonight, no matter by whose hand, she would hate Priest to the deepest hollow in hell.

"We let Chicorah lead this here thing," Lamarr said, "we gonna be doin' lots of sneaking about on our bellies past midnight, cutting throats in the dark."

"Luckily, we're not letting him lead it."

"He might have something to say about that."

"You guys always have something to say about everything."

Lamarr sat back with the rifle across his knees. "It's my suggestion, then—my strenuous suggestion, I might add—that we don't do none of that blazing-gun shit. I done some of that before, and it don't usually work out too well."

"No, I wouldn't think so."

"Well, then, we might want to get around to formulating a plan of one kind or another."

Priest thought he'd tell the truth and see how it went over. "I figured I'd ask Septemus nicely to turn over Dean and the workers who've been attacking the women. And then make an appeal for him and Griff to follow us back into town, turn themselves in, and confess to their general misdeeds, offenses, and all-around nastiness."

"Call it a hunch, but I don't exactly see events unfolding along those lines."

"Then we'll have to improvise."

That got a grunt. Lamarr had survived chains and war and killed anyone fool enough to try to rob him or brand him or lynch him. Three men this week alone, in fact. He didn't like deferring anything to Priest, who'd never even fought fist-icuffs much, but he'd let it all ride on for now until he disagreed.

"I still think I'd prefer to just strangle my daddy."

Priest saw it in Lamarr's face then, and knew Chicorah had been right about men who enjoyed their own suffering too much to allow it to end by their own hand. Lamarr would just as soon kill himself as he would Septemus. It would never happen.

But Priest only said, "Let's just see what happens when we get down there."

"Somebody coming."

It was easy to imagine an army of Apaches riding down from the rez, eager to go to war again against all the white-eyes, slithering on their bellies around the rancheria, no sound, perfectly patient, without fear. The truth of the matter was that they were well past the age of Cochise now, and the U.S. Army had decimated most of the renegade bucks. You had a broken people who were slowly starving and dying out, and it sometimes seemed even they were anxious for it to end.

Chicorah showed up with Delgadito and the two Mimbrenos who'd watched the store burn.

"The great Apache nation," Lamarr said.

Delgadito tried to match Lamarr's wide smile but couldn't get anything near as impressive. Delgadito couldn't take his eyes off Lamarr's yellow sombrero. "That is one fine hat."

"Thank you kindly."

"It is a proud day."

"And we might even get us some cake, too."

"Where's my grandfather?" Priest asked.

His gaze fixed on the hacienda, as if all his pride were wrapped up in the coming hours and he could make right what had gone so wrong, Chicorah said, "I brought him back safely. He was in your care."

"He left last night for White Mountain."

"He did not come."

Now, what the hell did that mean? Had Gramps gotten in trouble somewhere in town? Had his heart finally given out?

Lamarr said, "He's all right. He's just got hisself his own special kind of strategy."

Chicorah hadn't lowered his chin yet. He'd

waited half his life for a moment like this, when he could lead an attack against all the enemies of his people and burn his way into history. He was doing everything he could to carry an air of honor and death around him. Lamarr and Priest looked at each other. Chicorah's voice grew heavy with satisfaction and relief. "We will wait until the moon rises and begins to sink again."

"No. I'm going in to face the man who killed my mother and father. Now. And I want to see his face."

"No. I do not like this plan."

Priest should've expected something like this a lot earlier, but there was no going back. "It's not your place. You had no right to judge me before, and you have no right now. You presume too much, you said it yourself. I'm my own man."

Chicorah put his hand on Priest's shoulder, a firm grip, and one that told of violence about to come. The Mimbrenos both stiffened, and Delgadito made a face of intense pain because he did not want to hurt Lamarr, whom he'd loved a little ever since being outwrestled. Lamarr turned slightly in case he had to draw.

There was a moment when it could've gone either way, and nobody much gave a damn. They all had too many reasons for being here, one purpose just as good as the other. Odd that they should all be friends. Only Lamarr looked a little hesitant to start the killing now. He said, "Boys, ya'll gettin' a tad too touchy. How about we discuss this further?"

"We will have the ones who have hurt our women. We will torture them. That is our way."

"You can do what you like," Priest said. "I'd be thankful if you could start a ruckus in the camp, it'll make things easier for me. But I'm not waiting, and I'm not about to slit Yuma Dean's throat while he's sleeping. I want to see his face first. I'd rather die looking him in the eye. That's my way."

Chicorah lowered his chin and started becoming himself again. There was enough anger and murder to go around. "It is good."

They rode out to Septemus's hacienda, all six of them. Priest thought Chicorah and his men would break off and find another way in, but they stuck close, sitting high in the saddle. Lamarr drew up to a halt first outside the ornate wrought-iron gate that stood closed before the ranch. It was dark enough that no sentries had spotted them from far off, and the rain kept the rest of the hands in their bunks. Some had already headed off to Miss Patty's.

Cobb, the foreman, with a bandage swathing half his face, stood in almost the exact same place as he had on Septemus's birthday. Priest frowned, wondering when the hell the man ever actually did his job instead of waiting around the gate all the time. Another sentry was about to run off, but one of the Mimbrenos had him covered with his rifle.

The sense of being inside a closing circle came on strong. Cobb's hands didn't stray to his gunbelt and Lamarr wasn't smiling this time, the Winchester in the saddle boot close to his fist. Priest realized he had lived this moment before but knew it could not turn out the same way again.

Cobb decided to be stupid and tightened his shoulders. He ignored Lamarr and screamed at Priest. "You gonna pay for what you did to my mouth! It's all ruined, and I can't smile worth a good goddamn anymore. There's spaces now! I got to pay extra for a girl at Miss Patty's!"

"How much more?" Lamarr asked.

"Ten whole cents!"

"Well, hell, I'm in agreement with you. That there is an outrageous price for someone with only a couple holes in his mouth."

"I know it!"

Priest said, "I'm well acquainted with Miss Patty. I'll talk to her and see what I can do about getting you the regular price again."

Cobb let out a leer, and Priest shuddered. "You would?"

"Yep."

"Well, all right, then."

"Think you can open the gate?"

"What you want here?"

"To see Septemus."

The sentry was only a kid, seventeen or eighteen at the most, and still had too much to prove to the rest of the world. He hadn't been working on his sneer nearly as long as Sheriff Burke had been, but the results were about the same. "Mr. Hart don't truck with no Apaches or niggers."

"You'd be amazed," Lamarr told him, "at who that son of a bitch has truck with, boy."

Cobb started to flinch. "Ya'll get outta here now!"

"We've already been through this once, and you didn't wind up with too fair a shake and them there black eyes. How 'bout you just let us in quick-like this time and save yourself some sufferin'?"

"How 'bout I just kill you dead on your horse, nigger?"

Cobb reached for his pistol, and Lamarr drew and shot him in the face. Priest already had his gun on the boy, and he said, "Be smart and stay alive. Open this damn gate already."

"He's dead. You done killed Mr. Cobb!" The kid stood defiantly, thinking about going for the draw or maybe making a run for it, letting it course through his head a couple of times. Priest

241

thought he might make a go for it, and was forced to raise his Colt a little higher and point it directly between the kid's eyes before he made up his mind and opened the gate.

They rode in slowly, quietly. Even the gunshot had hardly seemed a whisper in the night with the rain coming down. Chicorah stared down at Cobb's corpse and said, "This might not be a bad plan after all."

"I thought you might like it once we got here."

The Apaches surrounded the kid, and Chicorah leaned over in his saddle and said something to him that Priest couldn't hear. Delgadito held his Burnside .54 carbine to the back of the boy's head, thumbing the hammer and tapping it against his skull until the kid finally sobbed something. Chicorah nodded, and Lamarr urged his horse forward. He stared down at the kid and said, "You're the lucky one. Remember that when you're achin' in the morning."

"Morning?"

Delgadito brought his rifle like a club and smacked the kid in the neck. Priest grimaced as he watched the boy twist in midair and hit the mud with a soft splat, rolling over once to lie still. He was facedown and bubbling in the muck. Priest was afraid he might drown if it puddled up too deeply. He got off his horse and left the kid in a sitting position beside the wall.

Priest turned to Chicorah and said, "What'd he tell you?"

"Only one man has been preying on the women. He told me his name and where he is on the ranch. We go to find him."

"Speaking of women, there are bound to be some here—and maybe children, too, I think."

Delgadito said, "You do not dictate to the son of Sondeyka."

"I'm not."

The water ran down the pointed angles of Chicorah's face, rivulets catching in the creases of his grim smile. They might not be fighting the U.S. Army or a warring tribe, but this was good enough for the time being. He said, "All I want is this man now."

"Good luck."

Priest watched the Apaches go, vanishing into the gray shadows and sheet rain. Lamarr turned to him. "You want to try the main house, the barracks, or that tiny version of the theater again?"

Dean wouldn't be in the regular cowhand quarters. They'd be talking business over bourbon. "I don't hear any music. Let's head to the house."

"Federales probably sent their wives and children home by now. Drink and enjoy themselves for a couple days before getting down to carving up the land and water rights and cattle."

They rode toward the main house of the hacienda. The rain drove down harder, until even the thunder was lost to the constant pounding and roar of water. Lamarr had to lean in close to Priest's ear. "What, you want to knock?"

"This is Sarah's house now."

"She ain't any more likely to enjoy seeing us tonight than Septemus will be."

"Put your gun away."

"The hell you say?"

"I don't want to start a shoot-out where she might be hurt."

"Exactly what kind of shoot-out were you considering?"

Priest hadn't thought it through enough. He'd let the signs take him too far without regard to consequences. He reached over and took the huge brass knocker in hand. It was cold enough to make him loosen his grip and suck wind through his teeth. He knocked twice.

"Good thing the Apaches ain't here to see this," Lamarr said, "knockin' on the enemy's door. They come out and shoot us, my dying breath will be I told you so."

"I bet it will."

Sarah answered.

She took one look at him and shook her head.

"You shouldn't be here, Priest McClaren, and ye mustn't stay."

He saw every mistake he'd ever made in her eyes, each regret and failure and lost chance. Jesus, he couldn't even take a step, the water slapping at his forehead like a thick, callused palm. He would've been pinned like that forever by the force of her glare, except Lamarr moved forward and carried him inside. He had to remember what he'd come for.

Priest had never been in the main house before and was awed by the wealth of what he saw: the European furniture, Oriental rugs, the portraits and chandeliers, the sheer magnitude of size and riches. He did not blame Sarah for being enraptured by this. He was only surprised it had taken so long.

"Get out of here now."

"Sarah—"

"You have no right—"

"Please . . ."

"And yer dripping on the carpets."

"Does Griff have a friend visiting him here?"

"And what business is it of yours?"

"It's Yuma Dean."

Finally, he had reached her. He couldn't do it with his love or his pleas, but somehow he had gotten to her with his need for revenge. Her face fell in along every beautiful curve and line. She said, "Yer daft—it's not possible."

"He came into town five years ago with Rafe and Griff to rob the bank. Griff stayed on." Priest listened hard and heard voices drifting from down the corridor. Laughter and liquor being poured, the titter of a woman.

"How can you be so certain?"

"Griff let it slip himself."

"Oh, my Lord. Oh, Priest." There, she'd lost the angry schoolmarm habit of saying his last name. "Leave. Leave now. You'll be killed otherwise. Go."

"Is he inside?"

"I won't tell you."

"Yes, you will, because no matter what's happened between us, you still won't harbor the murderer of my parents beneath your own roof. Now, where is he?"

"Don't harm my husband-to-be."

"Where is he?"

"Promise me."

"Sarah—"

"Promise me."

"*I swear.*"

Lamarr tried to get a warning hand on Priest, but he wasn't fast enough to quiet him. Priest's words rang along the corridor. Timing was everything and always would be. Gunfire exploded outside and they were into it.

"We're on our way," Lamarr said.

Priest met Sarah's eyes and gently pressed her forward to the stairwell. "Go upstairs now. Septemus won't be hurt." Lamarr could never let go of his pain and kill his short daddy, and Priest could never hurt Sarah that way. No matter who else might die, the bastard was going to make it out just fine.

Lamarr had already moved past him, drawing his gun and rushing down the hall, checking rooms and finding them empty, until they came to the study.

Septemus sat in a huge wing-backed leather chair, sipping sherry and dressed in his usual black trousers and purple shirt. A small fire burned in the fireplace, reflecting wildly across the room. The medals and buttons on his Confederate coat had been recently shined, and the tassels had been expertly cleaned. To his left sat a drunken woman, who still tittered although she was almost passed out.

Yuma Dean sat in a high-backed chair smoking a cigar and holding a whiskey. The image was too great to bear at once, and Priest had to look away, his newfound calm shattered now. His hair prickled and his clothes began to steam before the fire. His wet hair draped into his eyes. He had a long way to go. Was the knife in his hand?

He looked, and it wasn't. He drew his gun. He had to talk, to say his father's name, anything at all so Dean might understand, but Priest couldn't get the words out.

The only other person in the study was a Mexican general whose gaudy uniform had more epaulets, straps, emblems, and ribbons than Priest had ever seen on a man before. He must've been something big south of the border, all right. He stood up immediately and straightened his jacket and vest. "What is the meaning of this outrage? Explain yourself."

Lamarr said, "The padre and his uncle, Don Carlos Herrera Villejo, send their regards."

"What are you two doing here?" Septemus asked without the slightest trace of anger.

"Wanted to see if I could be your best man."

Priest wasn't about to let it go back and forth like this now, not about the wedding, not about Sarah.

More gunfire from outside rattled across the house. Griff wasn't in the room, and Priest spun, searching up and down the corridor. Men started to pour in the front door, running and shouting. Priest looked down the hallway and watched one of the vaqueros driven into the room by the blast of Delgadito's carbine. Blood splashed across a dining cart. Priest reached over and yanked Lamarr backward out of the study just as the general drew and fired his pistol. They fell against each other, scrambling along the wall, and Priest fired twice, aiming as far from Septemus as he could.

"You all right?"

"That Mex bastard done shot my hat!"

"Come on, there's no cover here."

"What we want with cover?"

"Griff's on the loose."

"Good point."

Shots twanged off the banister and tore great gouts from the wallpaper. Priest spun and saw another vaquero behind them, aimed, and shot him in the chest. The general ran in, followed by the giggling drunk girl and Septemus, who was brandishing his saber. Lamarr tossed Priest down, grabbed the edge of the oak dining table, and turned it on its side. It offered some cover, but not enough. The general fired twice more into the tabletop, cursing in Spanish. Septemus let out a growl that might've been laughter or impatience. The girl started clapping.

Lamarr said, "Have I mentioned this plan is for shit?"

"Wasn't my idea."

"Was too!"

The Apaches' singsong war cries filtered into the house through the open front door. Priest reached over the table and fired blindly twice.

Lamarr was thinking of making a run across the hallway and into the den, but he'd never make it. Priest was faster. He hunkered down, ready to rush, when a series of shots fired so fast into the table that they almost sounded like one large explosion. Chunks of wood spewed in every direction, and they both covered their eyes and ducked lower.

"Looks like Griff is here."

"Where's Yuma Dean?"

"Dunno."

Another door opened and slammed, and there was the sound of more running and shooting. Thunder warbled in the distance.

Priest figured what the hell and stood up, firing where he thought Griff would be. It was close. Griff lunged aside into the corridor, snapping off another shot. It caught the girl high between the shoulder blades and whipped her around twice on her toes before she crumpled.

Septemus was gone, but the general smiled, straightening his arm, sighting the pistol perfectly for Priest's heart. Now, already rising to his feet, Lamarr bore down on the General, but there wasn't enough time to do any goddamn thing.

A massive hand with hairy bulbous knuckles flashed out and descended over the Mexican general's head, covering his entire face. His muffled screams were cut short as he was lifted and dragged backward.

Wainwright loped easily across the floor, looking out from beneath his thick, high-ridged eyebrows so that his deep-set black eyes seemed like the gleaming gaze of an animal. His brutish three-hundred-pound body was incredibly graceful in its own way, as though he might be dancing with one of Miss Patty's girls, while those powerful arms descended and tightened around the officer until bones snapped.

Molly moved into view, pale and breathing hard, her gunbelt fastened to the last notch so it would hang freely below her belly. She stood before Griff, her hands loose at her sides. She winked at Priest. "Don't worry none about him."

"Jesus God," Lamarr said. "The sweet Lord done sent down angels to save us from that shitty plan!"

Griff snickered at Molly and said, "You gonna draw on me?"

She grinned and said, "I reckon."

"A girl like you ready to drop more kin in the mud? I'm gonna make you twice as dead as dead can get!"

He still wasn't any good at making a real threat, but he didn't mind at all as his mouth slid into a wild leer, drawing air for a nice big laugh.

Molly shot him in the teeth.

She groaned, her hands flashing out toward the wall to keep from falling. Her water had burst.

"I'm not all that fast really," she said, blood draining from her face as huge drops of sweat formed. "I just don't talk much."

"Molly!"

"Dean went out the back door. Get after him, Priest!"

Lamarr and Wainwright reached her. Priest hesitated for a second, then ran.

Chapter Seventeen

Unable to see in the lashing rain, Priest followed into the storm, hearing gunfire and watching some of the adobe buildings spilling smoke. The Apaches were still having fun, running Septemus's men to all ends of the camp. He passed three bodies lying in the mud, ducking flames and rushing in an almost straight line to the replica of the Home Hearth Theater.

He tried the back doors first, but they were locked. He worked his way around to the front of the building, grabbed the handle of the door, and pulled. Priest expected gunfire, but there was none. He checked behind him and spotted Chicorah sitting astride his horse in the distance, calmly watching. As if this wasn't difficult enough.

Muddy tracks soiled the doorway and floor. Priest stepped inside.

The footlights of the stage had been lit. Maybe Sarah was supposed to sing tonight for her husband-to-be, or they were to be entertained by some other show, maybe clowns carrying poodles, or magicians and their crippled birds. Priest moved among the aisles and seats, and the scuffs of dirt led him toward the stage. He'd drawn his gun, although he thought it was probably empty. That didn't matter.

Yuma Dean might be down in the orchestra pit, but more likely he was backstage in the dark. He was a runner and would've run as far as he could go—right there, in that corner behind some scenery designs and stacked boards. Septemus must've put on full productions of plays here and had acts from around the world come perform for him personally. Priest stepped closer, slowly, remaining out in the open. The footlights flickered and threw twining shadows around his feet. He scanned the stage but kept facing that black corner, already knowing how this had to play out.

Priest watched it going on before it even happened.

He holstered his empty pistol and began to

turn, showing his back to the spot where Dean crouched behind some free lumber. There was a swirl of breeze as Dean got himself clear and began to move. He came reaching forward with his left hand to pull Priest back by the collar, jamming the barrel of his pistol against the back of Priest's head with his other fist.

It was all right as long as Dean didn't immediately pull the trigger, and he wouldn't. He liked to snarl too much, get nose to nose. There was no reason for him to shoot, because he didn't know who else was out there in the night, or who else might be coming after him. He was safe for the moment and wouldn't want to alert anybody else to his position.

Now Priest just needed a little more room. Dean jabbed his pistol hard enough against Priest's skull to force him a step away, allowing him to turn around. That was enough.

"Who in the hell are you?" Dean asked.

Priest leaned in to get a good look, taking his time, making sure that after all this time he had finally caught up with the right man. Dean's eyes had a slight glaze to them, and he'd lost a lot of weight. His face remained soft as slime, those angles going wild, never meeting where they should have. Black dots speckled Yuma Dean's throat and wrists, pinhole scars from where he'd missed the vein. He was still using morphine, more than ever.

Something broke free inside Priest's chest, and the shock of it startled him. For a moment he felt five years younger, and all the events leading him up to this place were hard for him to track. There was a ridiculous bark of laughter, but Dean's soft mouth hadn't moved at all. Christ, Priest thought, that couldn't have been me. The sound came again and he reached up to touch his lips, feeling them drawn way back.

He quit smiling. "My name's Priest Mc-Claren."

"McClaren." Dean spun it over a couple of times. "You related to that little bitch who's been hunting after me?"

"Don't remember us?"

"Should I?"

"Wasn't that long ago." He held up Rafe's knife across the flat of his palm in a nonthreatening manner, like an offering. "How about this?"

"If you knew how many times I've been through questions like this, you wouldn't bother asking. 'You remember me? You remember my brother Johnny? You shot him down in Waco.' All you pups look and sound the same, so no, I don't remember a damn one of you."

Priest expected as much. "You called me Twitch."

"You look like a Twitch."

Maybe he did, but at least his hand was steady as iron. He kept waiting for the nerves to start flicking his last two fingers, but his flesh was cold and he didn't feel a thing anymore. "Bet you didn't forget my mother, though," he said. "You didn't like her looking at you."

"Don't like you looking at me neither, Twitch."

"She was deaf."

That got to Dean. All the bitter curves of his grimace suddenly snapped together. His head cocked and his gun dropped a few inches, then began to rise again.

It seemed to take him hours to lift it again. This was going to take a while. It wasn't the same gun—he'd stepped up to .45s. Dean had mended his ways some and kept these pistols clean, and they sparkled with the water on them reflecting the footlight flames. Molly should be here to see this ending, however it played out. Priest let out a sigh, knowing he was missing something.

All these years on his trail and the bastard comes right back to where he started it all with them, slipping in with ease. The .45 continued angling up, but Dean hadn't started to point it yet. Priest felt wet and wondered if he'd already been shot, but it was only the blood of his father hitting him again. The warmth nourished him this time, though—calmed him even more, if that was possible.

The wetness was gone and then it was there again, as if his father were being killed over and over, and each time the warmth gave Priest a little something extra, like another pat on the back. Papa saying, *I'm proud of you, son—what matters most is you finally made it here.* It could be true. Dean started to aim the pistol, his finger about to jerk. Priest kept expecting more, hoping beyond all reason, but he wasn't sure for what. It would come to him. The black empty mouth of the barrel looked no different from Dean's eyes. Priest smelled the lice-ridden clothes burning in the fireplace, Mother turning to look at Pa over her shoulder. Dean's finger clenching on the trigger. The voice of the child coming to him again, and perhaps it was Mother's and Papa's and Molly's too, everyone telling him not to get careless now. He had to hurry.

I was hoping this wouldn't be so easy.

Priest drove the blade through Yuma Dean's throat, and left it there.

Chapter Eighteen

Gramps sat in the study, smoking his pipe and sharing a bottle of bourbon with Septemus and Lamarr. Priest knew what must have happened. Deep in his head, Gramps had come to understand that he could do more good going white again and bringing Wainwright and Molly than he could do running around in a breechcloth.

Septemus Hart did not seem irritated in the slightest. His best men were dead, but whatever deals he had running with the Mexicans would still follow through. All the burned adobe on the rancheria would be rebuilt by the weekend. Every chip in the walls repaired, each piece of broken furniture replaced. A man like that didn't have to get angry if he didn't want to.

They'd achieved status quo again. The bodies had been dragged away and the Apaches had gone back to White Mountain with the man who had raped their women. They'd keep him alive for about a week.

Lamarr had taken his boots off and warmed his feet in front of the fire. This ranch was his legacy, and even if he'd never be declared an heir, he could at least enjoy its comforts for the time being. Septemus glanced over at him, maybe wanting to stab him through the heart, or maybe just wanting to put some of the past to rest. There'd be other days of fire and retribution like this, and more chances to beat the hell out of one another before Septemus owned up to the fact, or one of them finally got killed.

Priest found that Molly had been put to bed upstairs. Patty and Wainwright were both there, tending her. Patty said, "I knew this was a stupid idea, to have a pregnant girl riding all over creation in the middle of the night."

"So you came with them."

"You people needed one right mind among you. Fat Jim wanted to come, too, but I needed somebody to watch over the house."

Wainwright stared down at Priest, his hands speckled with dried blood, and said, "You should've asked for my help."

"I know."

"I wouldn't have let you down."

"You didn't."

"And don't worry, she's going to be fine."

"You ever do this before?"

"You work with twenty-five gorgeous ladies for a few years and you become an expert in such things."

Molly glanced up but didn't ask him if it was done. It had to be, or he wouldn't be here, she knew. Her face had some color back, but her breathing had grown even more shallow.

It seemed important that he at least ask the question that suddenly overwhelmed him. "Molly, tell me . . . who's the father?"

"I reckon two things about that," she said. Her gaze hardened, and he watched as she shifted beneath the blankets. She'd seen a lot of judgment on the trail and was ready for more. She waited.

Okay, so they were going to get into it. He had to say, "And what are they, Molly?"

"I reckon I don't know, and I reckon I don't care."

"I don't believe that."

"Good, I wondered how much credit you might furnish me."

"The hell does that mean?"

"I wasn't sure how much you'd heard about me, or what you believed."

"I know enough."

"And do you still love me?"

He pressed his hand to her belly, trying to touch the child breathing in there, feel the contours of its face. His thumb brushed back and forth. He could imagine a girl like Molly in there, without the rage or the inflamed need for revenge, waiting to be born so she could sit on a porch swing and drink sun-made iced tea with her beau beside her. It could happen. Mistakes could be mended.

"I love you, Molly. More now than ever."

He owed her everything.

Patty said, "It's time. Go downstairs, Priest."

He went. He sat in the study while Gramps and Septemus talked about water rights and land and the price of cattle. He drank whiskey, wondering if anything had been accomplished, and if he felt any different at all. Lamarr had fallen asleep, feeling at ease in his father's house.

Two hours later, he heard his sister screaming. He ran upstairs, threw open the door, and saw Molly thrashing in the bed. Patty looked horribly serious, and Priest knew something was wrong. Wainwright's shirtsleeves were rolled up to his elbows, and his massive arms looked too huge to handle the birth of a child. Priest felt the slow crawl of icy sweat bead across his upper lip.

"What can I do?" he asked.

"Nothing. Get out of here."

He didn't leave. He sat near the door, and after a time Sarah came in and sat beside him. They were both thinking the same thing, which was all they could think about at a time like this. If the child had lived, would they still be in love? He wanted to say something, but they both knew it would come out flat and meaningless. She tensed beside him, trying not to curl up in sympathy with Molly's pain. He took it on himself. "She'll be all right."

"Well, of course," Sarah said. "Any girl who can chase a wagon train of wanted men across the whole country can certainly bear her own child."

It sounded like it should be a mite easier than bringing down Sarsaparilla Sam, the one who liked to carve up women from the East. "God, I hope so."

"And you're in need of a larger family, Priest McClaren."

That stopped him. Was she saying she wanted to get married, have children of their own? He stirred and let the possibility lift him for a moment, but when he looked at her he realized that wasn't what she'd meant at all.

"I love you," he said.

"I know you do, and I loved you too, for a time, but that wasn't quite enough. Now, was it?"

"No."

He put his arm around her and hugged her close enough to press his face against her hair. He sniffed softly, and as she stood, he let her go.

"The baby is crowning," Wainwright said.

"The hell does that mean?"

"Its head is almost out."

Lamarr burst into the bedroom. He swept up behind Priest, and his smile, damn near larger than ever before, shone down.

Patty whispered in Molly's ear, giving orders, as his sister squealed and groaned, clawed the sheets, and pushed. Priest continued to watch, feeling detached from himself and the rest of the scene, witnessing the birth of his sister's child. Once the shoulders appeared the rest of the baby slid free effortlessly, a girl already breathing and making soft mewling noises.

"How is she?" Priest asked.

"Molly's fine. Your niece is perfectly healthy."

Lamarr frowned and said, "I don't see why you should be that baby's uncle any more than me."

"She's my sister."

"That's thin reasoning, I say. The baby's beautiful. I'm beautiful. Simple justice demands it. I should be her uncle."

Wainwright said, "Well, hell, if he's going to be an uncle, then I should be too. I'm the first one to ever hold her. I welcomed her into the world."

"You both will be."

"Well, all right, then," Lamarr said.

Patty cleaned and bundled the girl before handing her to Priest. He held the baby and brushed his lips against her fuzzy head.

She cried for a little while and then slept.

He did the same.

Behold a Red Horse

Cotton Smith

After the Civil War, Ethan Kerry carved out the Bar K cattle
spread with little more than hard work and fierce courage—
and the help of his younger, slow-witted brother, Luther. But
now the Bar K is in serious trouble. Ethan's loan was called
in and the only way he can save the spread is if he can drive
a herd from central Texas to Kansas. Ethan will need more
than Luther's help this time—because Ethan has been
struck blind by a kick from an untamed horse. His one slim
hope has come from a most unlikely source—another
brother, long thought dead, who follows the outlaw trail.
Only if all three brothers band together can they save the Bar
K . . . if they don't kill each other first.

___4894-9 $4.99 US/$5.99 CAN

Dorchester Publishing Co., Inc.
P.O. Box 6640
Wayne, PA 19087-8640

Please add $2.50 for shipping and handling for the first book and
$.75 for each book thereafter. NY and PA residents,
please add appropriate sales tax. No cash, stamps, or C.O.D.s. All
orders shipped within 6 weeks via postal service book rate.
Canadian orders require $2.50 extra postage and must be paid in
U.S. dollars through a U.S. banking facility.

Name_____
Address_____
City_____ State_____ Zip_____
I have enclosed $ _____ in payment for the checked book(s).
Payment <u>must</u> accompany all orders. ❑ Please send a free catalog.
    CHECK OUT OUR WEBSITE! www.dorchesterpub.com

COTTON SMITH
DARK TRAIL TO DODGE

Tyrel Bannon knows more about a plow than longhorn cattle, but the green farm boy is determined to become a Triple C rider on the long, hard drive from Texas to Dodge, the "Queen City of the Cowtowns." But this is a trail that only the brave, smart and lucky can survive. Waiting ahead are Kiowa warriors, raging rivers, drought, storms . . . and vicious rustlers out to blacken the dust with Triple C blood.

___4510-9 $4.50 US/$5.50 CAN

PRAY FOR TEXAS

COTTON SMITH

Rule Cordell is a pistol fighter, one of a special breed of warriors spawned by the Civil War, men with exceptional skill with the new weapon, the Colt .44 revolver. Like many other former Rebel soldiers, Cordell finds no place in the post-war world of bitter enemies and money-grabbing politicians, so he seeks refuge in bloody Texas and joins the band of guerrillas led by the wild and charismatic Johnny Cat Carlson. Cordell thinks he is fighting to bring freedom back to Texas, but he soon finds that Johnny Cat and his men are just outlaws out for all they can get. Now Cordell is ready to strike out on his own again, but the road to freedom will lead him through some hard choices and tough trouble. Before he can leave his past behind him, he'll have to face up to it, and the father who turned him to the gun in the first place.

___4710-1 $4.50 US/$5.50 CAN

DOUBLE VENGEANCE

John Duncklee

Joe Holly has his assignment. The army is sending him to Fort Huachuca, deep in the heart of Apache territory. It's no easy post. Apache raiding parties are a fact of life there, and the area is known for its thieves and hardcases. But they're the least of Joe's worries. His real mission at Fort Huachuca is a secret. He's working undercover to find out who at the fort is supplying information to the gunmen who have been robbing the army's payroll deliveries. He knows he can trust no one. He knows his life is on the line if he's discovered. What he doesn't know is just how many layers of lies and betrayal are waiting for him. He doesn't know yet—but he'll find out.

___4929-5 $4.99 US/$5.99 CAN

Dorchester Publishing Co., Inc.
P.O. Box 6640
Wayne, PA 19087-8640

GOLD
OF
CORTES

TIM McGUIRE

Amid the dust and desolation of southwest Texas lies a secret that has lasted for centuries—the hidden treasure of Aztec artifacts hoarded by Hernan Cortes. When Clay Cole finds English lord Nigel Apperson and Dr. Jane Reeves wandering the Texas desert, searching for the mythical prize, he agrees to sign on as their scout. Together they confront Texas Rangers, desperadoes, and the relentless Major Miles Perry, whose driving desire is to court-martial Cole for treason at Little Big Horn—treason Cole never committed. All that stands between them and the fortune of a lifetime is a Mexican revolutionary and renegade Comanches!